The Last Light of Aurethis

José F. Nodar

Camden Books Publishing

The Last Light of Aurethis / José F. Nodar
ISBN: 978-1-7643409-2-2 - Paperback
ISBN: 978-1-7645425-7-9 - E-Book

Dedication

In loving memory of my wife,

Miriam Vassallo Nodar,

and her enduring presence.

You are always in my thoughts.

For anyone who's ever loved deeply, lost fully, and still found

the courage to begin again.

Table of Contents

PROLOGUE

The Golden World

Aurethis was originally a vibrant world, a "song made of light."

Long ago, before the darkness and silence began, this planet shone brilliantly in space, resembling a glowing lantern. Its land was covered in shimmering, reflective sand, and its oceans perfectly mirrored the fiery light of its sun.

Everything on Aurethis, every individual's life, animal life, and particle essence, seemed aware that it was part of a sacred, living world, one whose pulse matched the rhythm of its slowly dying star.

Now, that heart trembled.

Each millennium, the light grew fainter, the day shorter, the glass rivers cooler. Yet the people of Aurethis refused to despair. Aurethis built, sang, prayed, and remembered. They remembered that living beneath a dying sun was not a tragedy, but purpose, and each dawn was a miracle they earned anew.

The Solenari — Keepers of the Last Light

On the high plateaus of Aurion's Belt, where the sun still burned brightest, lived the Solenari, those whom the planet called its first children. They believed the light itself carried memory, that within every golden ray danced the whispers of their ancestors, the laughter of lost generations, the promises of the dead.

Solenari cities could only be described as cathedrals of glass and mirror, and every morning, when the first light of dawn spilled across the horizon, the Solenari gathered on their terraces. They all opened their hearts and sang in harmonic resonance, deep, flowing chants that rippled through the air like sunbeams made sound. It was a deep, meaningful song.

They called it The Dawn Remembrance, their sacred ritual to remind the weary sun of its duty to rise, to be, to remember that they are Solenari.

The Solenari were a matrilineal people. At their heart sat the Lumen Mothers, wise women who interpreted solar flares as omens — bursts of divine speech written in fire across the sky.

Men served as artisans, shaping molten glass into luminous sculptures or maintaining the great Mirror Fields, where entire mountainsides glittered with sunlight refracted through mineral veins.

Their bodies reflected their devotion: bronze-hued skin that gleamed with a faint inner glow, golden-amber eyes elongated like liquid flame. Females shimmered like living prisms, honey gold at dawn, rose copper at dusk. Their movements were slow and ceremonial, every gesture a prayer.

When outsiders visited the high plateaus, they often shielded their eyes, for the brilliance of the Solenari cities was nearly unbearable.

Yet to the Solenari themselves, the light was not pain; it was home.

They had learned to love brightness the way others loved air.

"To hold the sun in our hands is not hubris," the First Lumen Mother, Eryna Solen, once said.

"It is remembrance made visible."

Their light endured for centuries — until others sought refuge from it.

The Varethine — The Shadow Walkers

Far below, where sunlight faltered and died against cliffs of obsidian, another people took root — the Varethine, dwellers of the twilight basins and endless caverns.

What a different race.

In their caverns, the air was cool and thick with mist, lit only by the pulse of bioluminescent fungi and the mirrored gleam of subterranean lakes; however, the Varethine did not curse the darkness.

They grew to embrace it, sculpting a world of quiet beauty beneath the surface.

While their homes were carved into stone walls, they had soft lights that pulsed through the tunnels like slow-beating hearts.

Every sound was sacred.

A reflection of something unseen.

To the Varethine, wisdom was not illumination but echo, and they firmly believed the planet itself whispered through vibration, that truth could be felt in the way sound touched stone.

Hence, they built vast chambers of reflection, and within them, they carved mirror-stones, crystalline tablets capable of capturing thoughts, dreams, and even emotions. Here, in these sacred chambers, the Varethine stored generations of memory within them, creating an underground archive of consciousness.

They were a democratic people, guided not by kings but by their Dream-Scribes. These Dream-scribes, mystics, interpreted visions seen in sleep as messages from the planet's soul. The Dream-Scribes were scholars and prophets both, their duty not to command but to listen.

In appearance they were as soft as shadow: lean and sinewy, their skin faintly translucent, their veins glowing blue beneath the surface. Their silver or violet eyes saw clearly in darkness. Females, shorter and elegant, bore moonstone skin that shimmered when they spoke, their throats glowing faintly with every word.

Where the Solenari bathed in sunlight, the Varethine dissolved into the dark. They moved like mist; their cloaks lined with reflective minerals that allowed them to disappear at will.

For centuries, tension simmered between light and shadow.

Yet war never came. The Solenari needed the Varethine's minerals for their mirrors; the Varethine needed Solenari light to power their deep tunnels.

Thus was born The Pact of Reflected Silence, a peace born not of love but of mutual necessity.

It was said that in the twilight halls, where the agreement was signed, no one spoke for an entire day. They simply watched each other's reflections flicker in a single beam of light that fell through a crack in the ceiling — and called it compromise.

The Aerethi — Children of the Sky Rivers

High above both light and shadow, suspended between them, drifted the Aerethi — the nomads of the upper atmosphere.

They lived on vast floating archipelagos tethered by crystal anchors to the magnetised winds.

To them, land was a memory, and movement was law.

The Aerethi cities were symphonies of motion, platforms woven of sky-silk and storm glass, airships gliding between them like silver birds. The air itself hummed with the resonance of wind-harps, instruments that captured the planet's breath and turned it into song.

They were traders and poets, couriers between the grounded and the buried, carrying Solenari mirrors, Varethine thought stones, and Thalanor metals across continents. Their proverb was simple:

"To drift is to live."

Every Aerethi birth was celebrated in storm.

A ritual all families did was to climb to the highest platforms and hold the newborn toward the roaring sky, naming them as lightning split the clouds.

Their society was clan-based, ruled by feats of courage performed in the tempest called Sky Deeds.

A pilot who repaired a storm anchor mid-gale or captured lightning in a forge crystal could claim leadership, if only until someone braver rose.

Their bodies bore the mark of the wind: compact and agile, pale golden skin that glowed faintly when charged with static, eyes white or sky-blue without visible pupils. Females seemed lighter than air, their hair flowing in perpetual motion. When excitement coursed through them, delicate tracings of lightning shimmered along their limbs like tattoos made of light.

To the grounded peoples, the Aerethi were unreliable — dreamers of sky and thunder. Yet to those who understood, they were the bridge between all worlds: light above, shadow below, flame on the horizon. Their laughter was rare; their courage constant.

"All suns die," sang Kael the Wind-Scribe, an ancient poet of their kind.

"But not all hearts remember how to fly."

The Thalanor — Harvesters of Ember Soil

Finally, the last clan was the Thalanor, who lived in the heart of the world, where molten sands hardened into crystal plains.

The Thalanor were a resilient people, known for two very basic things: they were the last to survive and the last to surrender. They flourished by finding life within decay, converting death into power.

Their home was the Aurethis desert, which glowed at night because of underground rivers of molten crystal. The Thalanor built massive bio-forges that channelled this deep heat to convert minerals and organic matter into energy. For them, their places of worship were also their farms, and their engines were also their sacred spaces.

The Thalanor clans believed existence was because of a transformation in which everything that burns changes, and everything that dies is reborn. When an elder neared death, they underwent "The Ember Rite"—they were consumed by fire on the sacred Ember Soil, and their energy fed new life and growth. This was a ritual of both farewell and continuation.

The people themselves reflected their forges.

The men were strong and broad, with mahogany skin streaked with visible glowing embers near their joints. Their deep bronze-to-red eyes looked like living flames. The women were statuesque, with skin dusted with metallic gold and eyes that held a fiery mix of dark and light. They wore beautiful yet tough, unyielding armour made from cooled, glass-like metal.

Every family kept a Flame Tree, a living sculpture grown from the ashes of their ancestors. At night, these trees glowed across the plains like constellations upon the ground — a Forest of the Dead, lighting the path for the living.

"What fades can be reignited," proclaimed High Forger Maen Thal,

The Last Light of Aurethis

"if the will burns brighter than the flame."

The Convergence — When the Sun Coughs

The world of Aurethis is ending.

The sun, which they call "The Sun Coughs," is weak, shaking like an old god.

It flashes brightly and then fades to a dull, sickly gold. The beautiful glass-skies are cracked and worn out.

Faced with this disaster, the four major groups try to find salvation.

- The Solenari: Build new light-filled temples, hoping to encourage the sun to recover.
- The Varethine: Dig deep underground, believing the answer lies in the planet's core.
- The Aerethi: Prepare "Sky Arks" (large ships) to escape the planet and find new stars.
- The Thalanor: Dig even deeper to build the massive "Heart of Ember," a planetary engine meant to re-fuel the dying sun itself.

Each group thinks its own solution is the only one, and they argue fiercely. But the sun's flares last longer, the nights get colder, and the storms are now terrifying.

The Last Alliance: The Golden Accord

When extinction is almost certain, four leaders from all four nations meet at a special spot called the Equinox Crossroads.

They vow that if Aurethis must die, some of its people will survive, carried by light to the stars. They believe that somewhere out there in the vastness of space another planet, a second sun, Illumeris, waits for them.

The four leaders meet and decide they must stand together—children of light, shadow, wind, and fire. They are resolute and radiant. Even if Aurethis is to die, its civilisation is to continue.

They will gather one thousand from each of their clans, the best of the best of Aurethis, and ensure that its people survive.

They make one ultimate promise:

"We were born of light. We will die as light. But somewhere our glow continues."

CHAPTER 1

The Gathering at aurion's Edge

The wind over the plateaus sang that morning—thin, brittle, almost metallic. Each gust carried dust that glittered like powdered glass, remnants of centuries-old light scattered across a world that had forgotten what true brilliance felt like.

Far below, the molten rivers of the equatorial plains had cooled to amber scars. The dying sun—Aurethis's first god and last tyrant—hung low and swollen, breathing a dull fire into the horizon. The sky shimmered like a cracked mirror, its once-eternal gold turned to weary brass.

At the cliff's edge stood the Glass Tower of Aurion's Edge, home of Lumera Sael, High Solar Engineer of the Mirror Temples, and the last scientist still capable of making sunlight obey. The tower's translucent walls bent the dim rays into slow rivers of colour that flowed across the floors, pulsing faintly like veins of living light.

Lumera herself stood on the balcony, tall and still as the tower that bore her name. Her burnished honey-gold skin glowed faintly, as if she absorbed what the sun could no longer give. Her eyes—liquid amber with mirrored pupils—reflected everything around her, including the fatigue she no longer admitted aloud. Silver-white hair, braided and threaded with copper wire, caught the faint breeze like strands of starlight.

For three nights she had not slept. The data was relentless: the solar decay had sped up beyond all prediction. What she once measured in centuries had collapsed to decades—and now, perhaps only years. In the labs below, her engineers whispered numbers that sounded like eulogies.

She thought briefly of her husband, Taren, tending the rooftop gardens above the tower. He was seventy-five now, still writing poems in the language of cartography—turning maps of light into elegies for a sun he once charted. She wondered if he felt the same quiet terror she did each dawn when the light returned thinner, paler, as if half-remembering itself.

Her daughters haunted her thoughts too. Mara, the physician, who had accused her of playing God. Aurek, her pragmatic son, who loved her yet distrusted her visions. And young Elen, her granddaughter, who filled secret journals with Lumera's forbidden formulas. They were all fragments of her— reflections bent at different angles.

"You were once our god," she murmured toward the fading horizon. "Now you are only a question I cannot solve."

A tone echoed through the tower—a long, descending hum that resonated in her bones. Someone was approaching.

From the east came the faint shimmer of movement against the clouded sky. A small craft sliced through the haze, its wings glowing with static light. The engines whispered, lightning coiled along the fuselage, and the glider landed on her balcony with a soft crack of thunder.

Tavir Kelen stepped out, shaking ozone from his cloak. Compact and agile despite seventy-one cycles, he looked carved from the same wind he rode. His pearly-tan skin glimmered faintly with bioluminescent veins that traced his neck and arms; his hair, a tangled white-gold, seemed perpetually in motion even when he stood still. His eyes—pale, pupil-less blue—sparked with restless humour.

He had been the Chancellor of the Sky Federation, the highest office among the Aerethi, yet no title could ever quiet his love of flight. "Stillness," he liked to say, "is where hope dies."

"By the winds, Lumera," he called out, laughing as he approached. "Your elevator hums louder than a thunderhead. Do all Solenari buildings sing now?"

"Only the ones that still listen," she replied with a weary smile.

Tavir grinned and clasped her hand. His palms were calloused—unusual for a politician, ordinary for a pilot.

Behind that grin, Lumera saw fatigue: the same kind that haunted her in mirrors. He had spent years fighting bureaucracy and physics alike, pleading for resources to finish the Sky Arks—the massive vessels meant to ride the dying winds to another star. His own family had fractured under the weight of that duty: Nivara, his storm-navigator wife, still loyal but distant; Ryn, the rebellious son who accused him of cowardice; Tahlia, the diplomat daughter who followed him out of love and pity; and Mira, the youngest, who sang the skies into memory.

Tavir was both leader and exile of his clan, a man whose dreams had outflown the patience of his people.

A chime announced a second arrival. The tower's inner door opened, releasing a faint echo of subterranean air—cool, mineral, and damp with the scent of earth.

Kaedon Vareth stepped through, his long coat whispering across the glass floor. Lean and pale, with veins that glowed faintly blue beneath his translucent skin, he carried an aura of quiet gravity. His silvery-grey eyes, reflective as still water, seemed to see everything and judge nothing. Black hair streaked with white fell loosely around his shoulders.

The Varethine writer and Dream-Scribe Laureate of Thrayne had journeyed from the depths of the planet's twilight basins, leaving behind his wife, Evara, and their quiet life among the echo pools of the Obsidian Archive. There, thoughts were carved into mirror-stone, and every whisper became a record. His daughter Lynis, blind but prophetic, had once told him that his path would end "where the glass remembers the sun." That was why he came.

"Still chasing sunlight, Lumera?" he asked gently.

"Still hiding from it?" she countered, smiling for the first time in weeks.

Kaedon bowed slightly, every movement deliberate, poetic.

"The light grows fainter, yet the silence grows wiser," he said. "Perhaps both are necessary."

Tavir snorted. "Leave it to a cave-dweller to make extinction sound philosophical."

Kaedon's lips curved faintly. "Words are all that remain when fire forgets us."

Lumera felt the familiar warmth of old friendship—the comfort of arguments that had survived decades. But as the elevator hummed again, the air thickened with heat, heavy and metallic.

The last to arrive was Sera Thal, High Flame Keeper of Dravonar. The doors opened to a gust of warm air that smelled of iron and spice. She entered with the unhurried grace of a mountain, her mahogany skin glowing from within like living coal. Her eyes burned bronze-orange, steady as forge fire. Curls of red-gold hair cascaded over her shoulders, a halo of embers that never cooled.

She leaned on a staff of tempered glass-metal that still radiated heat, and when she spoke, her voice carried both command and compassion.

"You speak of dying," she said, her tone rich and deep, "but what if the sun need not die at all?"

Lumera smiled faintly. "You came through the ash fields?"

"The forges demand it," Sera replied. "The Heart of Ember trembles. Its core is fracturing. My priests call it divine wrath. I call it instability."

Behind that strength, Lumera sensed the sorrow Sera never spoke of—the lingering shadow of her husband Varen, lost decades ago in a forge explosion that birthed her faith in renewal. Her son Jonar had inherited his father's brilliance but none of his warmth, obsessed now with preserving the forges at any cost. Her daughter Danea, gentle and defiant, had turned compassion into rebellion, preaching love where doctrine demanded order. Even Sera's grandchildren were split between flame and flight: Eris, the runaway who sought freedom among the Aerethi, and Karo, the quiet boy apprenticed to Lumera herself.

Sera had the look of a woman who had given everything—except her will.

The four elders stood together in the tower's heart: light, shadow, wind, and flame reunited after half a century apart. The mirrored walls caught their reflections and wove them into one shifting image—a tapestry of age and endurance.

They had first met as children during the Solar Convergence Festival, the last day Aurethis had known full light. Four youths from different worlds, drawn together by curiosity and the reckless promise of friendship. They had sworn, hands clasped beneath the blazing sky, that if ever the sun forgot them, they would remember it for him.

Now they kept that promise.

Lumera touched the crystal console. The room dimmed, leaving only the central table glowing with the holographic projection of the dying sun. Patterns of flare and decay pulsed like a weakening heartbeat.

"This is what remains," she said quietly. "The core temperature is collapsing. The sun will implode within the next decade—perhaps sooner. The Mirror Temples cannot compensate. The planet will freeze from the inside out."

Kaedon's eyes flickered. "The stories were right then. The end will come not with fire, but silence."

Tavir's jaw tightened. "The Federation calculated forty years. I built my entire evacuation schedule around that."

"Then you built it on faith," Lumera said. "The numbers no longer obey optimism."

Sera leaned forward, planting her staff on the glass. A ring of heat radiated outward, shimmering in the hologram.

"The Heart of Ember was our answer," she said. "We thought to feed the sun with the planet's molten blood. But the crust resists. The forges fracture. It is as though the world itself refuses to die for us."

Kaedon loosened the cloth bundle he carried. "Perhaps it should not. Perhaps our task is not to keep the sun alive, but to remember it."

He unwrapped a black obsidian slab etched with a pictorial figure that caught the dying light.

"The Mirror Code," he explained. "A resonance pattern found in the oldest Varethine dream-records. It speaks of a twin flame—another sun, another home. The myth of Illumeris."

Lumera's eyes widened. She drew from her sleeve a triangular crystal, its surface alive with faintly pulsing lines.

"Then it may not be a myth at all. I found these coordinates hidden in the solar flare data—too structured to be noise. I thought they were corruption. Now I think they're an invitation."

Tavir circled the table, lightning crawling faintly across his fingertips. "A map," he murmured. "A map of where the light remembers itself."

Sera's voice softened. "To the Second Sun."

The room fell silent. Outside, the horizon flickered as if the dying star had overheard its own eulogy. The mirrored walls shimmered; for a heartbeat, all four elders appeared younger— four children standing beneath the first sky.

Then the vision passed.

Lumera clenched the glowing shard in her fist.

"Four people," she said. "One thousand souls besides our own families. Each of us must choose one thousand from our own to carry this light into the dark. If we fail, Aurethis dies forgotten."

Sera lifted her staff. "And if we succeed?"

Kaedon's eyes met hers, calm and luminous. "Then somewhere, our glow continues."

The wind outside rose, swirling through the mirrors until the entire tower hummed like a giant instrument. The dying sun flared one last weary time, flooding the chamber in molten gold.

And in that light, the four elders—scientist, writer, politician, and priest—stood not as relics of old worlds but as the architects of a final dawn.

Aurethis might die, but its children were not yet ready to let the light go.

CHAPTER 2

Echoes of Childhood Light

There was a time when Aurethis still sang.

The air was clear, the sky a sea of molten gold, and the sun, young, and fever-bright, shone without falter.

It was the day of the Solar Convergence Festival, the only day when light touched every corner of the planet, from the highest mirror fields to the deepest caverns.

Once in every thousand cycles, the planet's rotation, tilt, and orbit aligned perfectly, and the world became one gleaming sphere of illumination.

The Solenari called it The Day of Memory.
The Varethine called it The Day of Truth.
The Aerethi called it The Wind of Joining.
And the Thalanor called it simply the Ember's Breath.

It was the day the four first met.
Long before titles, before vows, before the sun began to cough itself to death.

The Plateau City of Aurion's Edge shimmered that morning as if the gods themselves had taken residence. Rivers of reflected light flowed between towers of crystal and glass. Choirs of Solenari children sang on terraces, their harmonic chants rising like vapor to the heavens.

At the city's centre, in the Grand Plaza of Mirrors, the world gathered. Delegations from all four nations stood together, rare and uneasy.

The air smelled of ozone, molten sand, and fruit steeped in sunlight.

Amid the endless brilliance, four children stepped into the plaza's heart, strangers, yet somehow familiar.

Lumera Sael was twelve cycles then, all sharp eyes and questions. She wore a simple robe woven with thin silver threads, though her hair already shimmered with the white that marked her bloodline.

She had been chosen as the Solenari Delegate of Youth to recite the Dawn Hymn before the assembled crowds, which was an honour usually reserved for adults.

Her mother had wept at the announcement; her father had cautioned humility. But Lumera, even at twelve cycles, was certain that the sun understood pride.

While others rehearsed chants, she studied the mirrors, fascinated by how light curved across their surfaces. She saw patterns there — equations the priests ignored. It was then she noticed the boy standing beyond the edge of the ceremony, watching the reflections with quiet intensity.

He was Kaedon Vareth, age of ten cycles, son of a Varethine sculptor.

Unlike the others of his kind, who wore cloaks to shield from the light, he had removed his hood.

His pale skin gleamed faintly, veins glowing soft blue.

He had never seen such brightness before.

The Varethine rarely left their caverns; the sun above was spoken of like a storybook creature.

Beautiful, terrible, possibly a myth.

But his father had insisted he witness the Convergence.

Kaedon squinted at the radiance, blinking tears.

The light hurt him, yet he found it intoxicating. For the first time, shadow had nowhere to hide, and neither did he.

Lumera approached, curious.

"Does it blind you?" she asked.

He shook his head slowly.

"No. It reminds me of how much of the world I've never seen."

"You're not supposed to look directly at it," she warned.

"Then why build towers made of mirror?"

She had no answer, and for that reason, she liked him instantly.

A burst of laughter rippled through the plaza as a gust of wind tore a streamer from one of the upper terraces, sending it tumbling through the air like a ribbon of flame.

A figure leapt from a railing to catch it.

A blur of motion, white hair flashing, cloak billowing.

He landed effortlessly near them, grinning like someone born of mischief and gravity both.

Tavir Kelen, who was eleven cycles old, child of the Aerethi wind clans, had arrived from the upper atmosphere the day before. Everything about him moved.

His eyes, his hands, even the way he breathed. He wore storm glass rings that hummed faintly with static, and his laughter made the air crackle.

"You two look like statues," he said, tossing the streamer back toward the crowd. "Are all ground-dwellers this solemn?"

Lumera bristled. "We are not ground dwellers. We are Solenari. We build light."

"You trap it. We ride it." Tavir countered.

Kaedon tilted his head. "Ride the light?"

"The wind is light. You just haven't learned how to see it," Tavir said, winking.

It was nonsense, of course.

And yet, even then, something about the boy's confidence made the impossible feel like physics waiting to be proven.

A sudden tremor interrupted their argument beneath their feet.

Not a quake, but a deep, rhythmic thrum, like a heartbeat rising through stone.

The crowd quieted.

The surrounding temperature grew warmer.

The Thalanor had arrived.

From the southern gate marched a delegation of flame-bearers, their bronze banners rippling in the heat. At their centre walked Sera Thal, thirteen cycles, the eldest of the four, already tall, broad-shouldered, and self-assured. Her dark skin shimmered with gold dust; her red-gold hair caught the sunlight and turned it into fire.

She carried a ceremonial brazier. A living flame drawn from the Ember Plains. The crowd parted as she passed, the air shimmering around her.

She set the brazier in the plaza's heart, opposite the mirror altar.

Fire met reflection, and for the first time, light and flame danced side by side.

Lumera watched in fascination.

"You brought fire to a place of mirrors," she said.

"And you built mirrors in a world of fire," Sera replied.

"Seems we understand each other."

Kaedon bowed slightly.

"The Varethine say the flame is the sun's echo, trapped beneath the skin of the world."

Sera smiled. "Then perhaps today the world will answer back."

When the ceremony began, the four of them were instructed to stand together at the centre of the plaza, representatives of the future, embodiments of unity.

The priests and emissaries surrounded them in concentric circles.

The High Lumen Mothers chanted, their voices merging into a low harmonic drone. The mirrors around the plaza shifted in perfect synchrony, bending sunlight into a spiralling column that ascended into the sky.

It was said that during the Convergence, the sun could hear.

And perhaps it did, for the air itself seemed to vibrate with life.

The glow was so intense that the glass beneath their feet melted into shallow pools.

Lumera felt it first.

The strange awareness that the light was alive.

Kaedon heard it as a sound just beyond the threshold of hearing. The hum of a word that had no tongue.

Tavir felt it in his blood, a current pulling him skyward.

Sera saw it reflected in the flame she carried, the fire twisting into shapes that almost seemed to listen.

Something vast and wordless passed through them.

A presence, a pulse of understanding.

Later, Lumera would call it resonance.

Kaedon would write that the sun "looked at us and remembered itself."

Tavir would say it felt like standing inside the breath of creation.

Sera would never describe it, only bow her head whenever someone spoke of it.

That night, after the ceremonies ended, and the delegates retired to their quarters, the four children slipped away from their chaperones.

They met on the highest terrace of the Mirror Temple, where the air still shimmered with residual light.

The sky had turned a pale violet, the sun settling behind the horizon like an ember refusing to fade. For the first time, stars were visible—tiny sparks against the golden haze.

"Do you think it will always be this way?" Lumera asked quietly.

Kaedon looked up. "Everything ends. But endings are only places where memory begins."

"Spoken like a Varethine," Tavir teased. "I say the sun will live forever, because I plan to race it."

Sera chuckled, setting down her brazier.

"And I say we should be grateful to live beneath it, however long that may be."

The four of them stood together, watching the last light shimmer across the mirror plains. The reflection painted their youthful faces in gold and rose.

Lumera raised her hand, palm glowing faintly in the dusk.

"Then let's promise something. If the sun ever forgets us, we'll remind it who we are."

Kaedon placed his slender hand over hers.

"We will write it in light and shadow."

Tavir added his, a spark dancing between their fingers.

"We will carry it in the wind."

Sera placed hers last, warm and steady. "And we will keep it in the fire."

The air trembled, as though the planet itself heard. A single beam of lingering sunlight stretched across the horizon, touching their joined hands.

It was the last full Convergence Aurethis would ever see.

Decades later, when the sun failed and their world grew old, each would remember that moment differently. Lumera would recall the warmth on her palm. Kaedon would remember the echo that lingered in the air. Tavir would remember the taste of ozone and youth. And Sera would remember how the flame in her brazier had bent toward Lumera's mirror and, for a heartbeat, had become one with it.

They had not known it then, but the vow made beneath that violet sky had bound them tighter than blood.

And now, fifty years later, as the planet trembled, and the sun gasped its last light, they had come together again to honour that promise.

To remind the heavens that Aurethis still lived, still remembered, still burned.

CHAPTER 3

The Dimming Sun

The third dawn after the gathering was colder than any Lumera Sael could remember. The sun rose late, dragging itself over the horizon like a wounded animal. Its light no longer poured—it trickled, thin and pale, turning the glass fields below into dull copper. For the first time in living memory, the shadows did not retreat; they lingered stubbornly, stretching like long fingers across the plateau.

From the upper balconies of the Glass Tower, Lumera watched the day hesitate.

Even the air had changed. The winds carried a faint metallic scent, sharp and bitter—the smell of dying photons. Instruments in her laboratory chimed warnings in a chorus of soft, mournful tones.

When she placed her hand upon the console, the surface trembled beneath her touch. The readings were worse than she had feared. The solar flares had weakened again; the star's magnetic lattice had collapsed by another fraction. What should have taken decades was happening in months.

The sun of Aurethis was unravelling.

And with it, everything they had ever been.

By the time the other three arrived in the observatory, Lumera had already assembled the projection. The central chamber glowed dimly, filled with floating ribbons of light that mapped the star's decaying pulse. It flickered in rhythm, a heartbeat slowly losing sync.

Sera Thal entered first, her presence filling the impersonal space with warmth. She set her ember staff beside the display and leaned forward, the glow of her eyes reflecting the dying star.

"You summoned us before the second bell," she said, her tone half concern, half knowing. "You haven't slept again."

"There's no time for sleep," Lumera murmured.

The door slid open with a soft sigh, admitting Kaedon Vareth, silent as dusk. His cloak shimmered faintly with dust from the caverns; the faint glow beneath his skin pulsed in steady contrast to the flickering hologram.

"It is worse," he said quietly. "I felt it even in the tunnels. The ground hums differently now. The light from above tastes...thin."

Tavir arrived last, in a burst of ozone and static, shaking frost from his sleeves. His flight harness still hissed with cooling air.

"You were right," he said to Lumera. "The upper winds are dying. The ion belts are collapsing—our Sky Arks can't catch enough current to stay aloft much longer."

"Then we've begun to fall," Sera said.

No one answered her.

Lumera expanded the hologram. The image of the sun filled the chamber—a sphere of trembling gold streaked with veins of dark matter. At its poles, great scars pulsed faintly.

"This," she began, her voice measured, "is the spectrographic data collected over the past thirty cycles. These fluctuations here—" she gestured toward the black fissures "—represent the decay of the outer plasma shell. In simple terms, the sun's skin is peeling away. The core temperature has fallen by twelve percent since the last Convergence."

Tavir exhaled softly, running a hand through his white-gold hair. "Twelve percent? That's impossible."

"Impossible is what the universe calls temporary," Lumera replied.

Kaedon stepped closer. "How long before the collapse becomes irreversible?"

Lumera hesitated. The room dimmed slightly, as though the question itself carried weight.

"Months," she said finally. "Maybe a year, if the next flare holds."

The silence that followed was not empty—it was dense, thick with the sound of realisation. The end of their world had ceased to be prophecy. It was now arithmetic.

Sera was the first to speak again.

"Then the Heart of Ember must be ignited now. We have enough molten feed to sustain fusion for another century if we channel it through the crustal veins."

Lumera turned to her. "You would drain the planet's mantle? That heat keeps your people alive. It powers every forge, every harvest, every home in Dravonar."

"And what use is warmth to the dead?" Sera snapped, then softened. "If the choice is between extinction and sacrifice, I will burn what remains. Faith without flame is ash."

Tavir slammed his palm on the console. "Faith won't launch ships! We barely have three operational Sky Arks. The others are grounded, and the Federation has seized our fuel reserves. They think the sun's decay is temporary—another cycle. If I defy them, I risk civil war before the planet even dies."

"Then defy them," Lumera said simply.

He glared at her. "Easy for you to say from your tower of mirrors."

"And easier still," she returned sharply, "to watch from the sky while the world beneath you burns."

The room crackled.

Literally.

Sparks leapt from Tavir's fingers, scattering like tiny bolts across the floor. Sera moved between them, her heat neutralizing the charge.

"Enough!" she said. "We are not enemies."

Kaedon's calm voice broke the tension. "Perhaps not enemies—but we have become strangers to one another's fears." He touched the edge of the projection. "Each of us speaks for a dying people. None of us can save them alone."

Lumera exhaled slowly, forcing the anger from her chest. "Then we must save what we can. I've been working on something—a plan that began as a myth."

She reached into her sleeve and withdrew the triangular crystal she had shown them before. It pulsed faintly, echoing the rhythm of the holographic sun.

"This contains data from the Mirror Temples—light codes hidden in the solar flares. I believe they are coordinates embedded patterns left behind when the star was still stable. But they don't align with any known system."

Tavir frowned. "Coordinates to where?"

"I don't know," she admitted. "But they match the resonance frequencies Kaedon found in his Mirror Code. The probability of coincidence is infinitesimal."

Kaedon nodded, producing his obsidian slab. The amulet shimmered faintly, harmonizing with Lumera's crystal. "In the ancient dream-archives, there is mention of a twin sun—Illumeris. A place where the first light fled when ours faded. The myths say it exists 'beyond the rivers of stars.'"

Tavir rolled his eyes. "So, we're chasing bedtime stories now?"

"Perhaps stories are all we have left," Kaedon said gently. "They are the scaffolding upon which hope is built."

Sera regarded the two artifacts. "Light and shadow, reflection, and flame. Perhaps the universe speaks through us after all."

Lumera's expression softened. "If these coordinates are real, they might lead us to a world capable of sustaining life—a second Aurethis."

"And if they lead nowhere?" Tavir asked.

"Then we die trying to remember what it meant to live."

For a moment, the weight of those words pressed down on them like gravity.

Outside, lightning rippled across the sky—slow, heavy arcs that moved with the lethargy of exhaustion. The tower's mirrors flickered, unable to hold a steady reflection.

Kaedon broke the silence first, his tone quiet but resolute.

"Then we must begin the Golden Accord anew. One thousand from each clan. The best, the brave, the foolish enough to believe in tomorrow. Four thousand souls to carry our story. Four thousand."

Sera nodded. "The Heart of Ember can provide launch power, but we must divert its energy carefully. Too much, and the crust will rupture."

"The Sky Arks," Tavir muttered, rubbing his temples. "I can hide three in the shadow currents. They'll be invisible to Federation patrols. But I'll need fuel. The Thalanor could provide heat plasma if—"

"If you stop stealing our resources," Sera interrupted dryly.

He grinned, weary but genuine. "Borrowing. Temporarily."

Kaedon smiled faintly. "You two argue like elements in balance."

Lumera deactivated the projection. The room darkened, leaving only the faint glow from the instruments and the ember of Sera's staff.

"Then it's decided," Lumera said. "Each of us will return to his or her people. Choose those who will go, prepare those who will remain. When the next flare cycle begins, we meet again—at the Equinox Crossroads."

"And if one of us fails?" Tavir asked.

"Then the rest continue," she replied. "The light doesn't wait for certainty."

Sera reached across the table and placed her hand over Lumera's. Her palm was hot, almost burning. "You were always the one who saw the path before the rest of us. Just remember, light cannot exist without shadow—or it burns itself blind."

Kaedon added his hand, cool and steady as stone. "And shadow cannot breathe without flame."

Tavir hesitated, then placed his over theirs, a faint hum of static joining the warmth. "Nor can the wind carry memory without both."

Lumera closed her hand over the crystal between them. The four elements—light, shadow, flame, and air—met, merged, and for one heartbeat, the tower hummed like a living thing.

Outside, the dying sun flared once, sudden and violent, a convulsion of energy that bathed the horizon in blinding gold. The entire world seemed to pause, suspended in that radiance.

When the flare faded, the chamber was silent once more. The projection had died; its light extinguished.

But on the floor, burned into the crystal surface, was a faint new mark: two interlocking spirals—the symbol of the twin suns.

They looked at one another. None spoke the word aloud, yet each knew it.

Illumeris.

The Second Sun.

Their destination, their myth, their ultimate gamble.

That night, as the others slept in the tower's guest chambers, Lumera remained awake in her observatory. She stood before the viewport, the crystal shard warm in her hand. Far below, the molten veins of the planet pulsed faintly in sympathy with the dying sun.

She thought of her family—the estranged daughter in the clinics; the son labouring at the Mirror Forge; her granddaughters dreaming of escape. Would they forgive her for abandoning them to chase a legend?

She pressed her hand against the cold glass. The reflection of her face merged with the faint flare of the sun outside. For a moment, she saw both herself and something vast—an echo of the promise she had made as a child under the first full light.

"We will remind the sky who we are," she whispered.

The light answered with silence, but in that silence, she thought she heard it breathing.

The sun dimmed.

The tower hummed.

And somewhere deep within its glass bones, Aurethis counted its last days.

CHAPTER 4

Secrets in the Flame

The journey home began under a veil of ash.

Sera Thal left the glass tower before sunrise, riding a heat-skiff that skimmed the cooling currents along the plateau's edge. The wind bit cold, but the skiff's belly burned with a steady glow that kept frost from settling on the rails. Behind her, the mirrored heights of Aurion's Edge dimmed and fell away; ahead, the horizon reddened—the equatorial plains stirring like a magnificent animal in uneasy sleep.

As she descended, the air changed. Ozone gave way to the iron-sweet breath of furnaces; the sky's brass softened to ember. When the first low dunes appeared, their crests glimmering with embedded glass, she felt the familiar ache in her chest ease. This was home: the scorched belt of Dravonar, where the soil remembered every footfall and the wind carried the taste of work.

The heat-skiff banked once and settled onto the sky dock carved into the city's flank. Ember City spread below her like a constellation—thousands of forges, workshops, and heat wells pulsing in an orchestral rhythm, a heartbeat that belonged to both people and stone. Between them, the Flame Trees of the Thalanor stood in courtyards and alleys, their glassy trunks glowing softly with the living memory of ancestors. At night, the trees would turn the whole city into a forest of stars.

Sera disembarked to a wave of warmth that kissed her cheeks. The dockhands straightened as she passed, palms pressed to chest in the old salute. She returned the gesture, but her mind stayed with the image of the dying sun floating above Lumera's table—those black fissures looking like spiders through gold like grief through a heart.

A messenger waited at the lift: a young acolyte with soot on her face and reverence in her eyes.

"High Flame Keeper," she said, breathless. "The Council has convened. They await you in the Temple of Vessels."

"Tell them I'll join them after I've washed," Sera answered. "And send for my children. Both."

The acolyte bowed and fled.

Alone in the lift, Sera touched the warm glass rail and closed her eyes. She let the city's music rise through her— bellows sighing, gears whispering, anvils speaking in sparks. In that steady, familiar symphony, she felt the shape of the choice before her grow razor clear.

We will ignite the heart, she thought. And with it, we may end our own.

Her residence wrapped around a central heat well—a circular core where amber light climbed in slow spirals. The walls bore metalwork from three generations, her grandchildren's first hammer marks standing proudly beside Varen's delicate wire filigrees. His touch lingered everywhere: on the lift's handrail, burned smooth by his palm; in the hairpins still resting on her vanity; in the bench that creaked in precisely the same way when she sat to remove her boots.

She bathed quickly, sluicing the dust of travel from her skin with heated mineral water. In the bright pane above the basin, her reflection burned back at her—mahogany and ember, bronze eyes steady. Varen would have teased her for the set of her jaw; he had always told her she wore conviction like armour. Arch-Priestess of Stubborn, he used to say, pressing a kiss to that very jaw. The only fire I've never tamed.

She was fastening her red-gold curls with tempered pins when the door chimed.

Danea entered first, her movements quiet, hands clean despite the hour. Healer's hands. Compassion had taught them patience; burden had taught them strength. She stood with the weight of many last goodbyes on her shoulders, her copper-brown eyes soft and unguarded.

Behind her came Jonar—all edges and heat. The engineer's cloak hung heavy with forge dust, and the orange burn of sleeplessness lit the rims of his eyes. He did not kiss his mother's cheek. He bowed, formal as a blade.

"You sent for us," he said.

"I did." Sera gestured toward the low table beside the heat well. "Sit, both of you."

Jonar stayed standing.

Danea sat and took Sera's hand.

"I've returned from Aurion's Edge," Sera said. "The news is worse than our last projections. The sun's decay is... accelerating. Dramatically."

Jonar's jaw tightened. "How dramatically?"

"Months," Sera said. "A year, perhaps. Not decades."

The room contracted. Even the heat seemed to draw back. Danea's breath stuttered; Jonar's gaze sharpened to a point.

"Then it's as I feared," Jonar said, voice flat. "We must seal the southern vents, divert the mantle feed, and increase output to the Heart of Ember by thirty percent. We can sustain planetary radiance long enough to stabilize the outer shell."

"And rupture the crustal veins in the attempt," Sera returned. "Do you think I do not know the figures? I carried them in my bones across the ash fields."

He flinched, anger as a reflex. "This is not about feelings, Mother. The Heart can work. If we starve it now—"

"Starve?" Danea's voice, usually gentle, sharpened. "Jonar, we are speaking of draining warmth from homes, from gardens, from hospitals. This is not just power. It is life."

"It is life," he agreed tightly, "which is why we give more to the Heart that can return it."

"And if it cannot?" Sera asked.

Silence. In it, Sera heard the truth Jonar would not say: that no metric promised salvation, only deferral.

Sera turned her hand palm-up on the table. "I met with the others. Lumera. Tavir. Kaedon. We have a plan. One chance of carrying our people's memory into a sky that may still receive it. We will select four hundred—one hundred from each nation—and launch them on the Sky Arks toward a second sun."

Danea exhaled, grief and relief braided. "Then there's hope."

Jonar let out a short, incredulous laugh. "Hope?" He looked at Sera as if he did not know her. "You would burn the Heart to throw a handful of lives at a myth."

Sera held his gaze. "Not a myth. A map. The Mirror Temples hold light codes in the flare patterns. Kaedon found a concordant frequency in the oldest dream-stones. The coordinates align. We are not leaping into a void, Jonar. We are following the echo of a promise older than our languages."

"I have no use for echoes," he hissed. "I am an engineer. I have a use for heat."

The heat well flickered, a slight tremor at the edge of perception. Sera felt it in her bones—the same irregularity she had felt in the tower. The city's pulse had missed a beat.

She rose. So did Jonar, compelled by old reflex to match her height.

"I called you here," Sera said, "because there is more you must know." She looked at Danea, then back to her son. "For the past twenty cycles, I have been diverting a portion of the Heart's yield into sealed capacitors beneath the southern ridge."

Jonar went still.

"Diverting," he repeated softly. "Into what?"

"Launch capacitors," Sera said. "Conduits that can be reconfigured into a catapult array when the time comes. The Heart of Ember can prime the Sky Arks—once. Perhaps twice. After that, the system will fail." She did not look away. "It is our only way off this world."

Jonar's cheeks flushed; the ember-lines beneath his skin smouldered. "You stole energy from our forges. From our people. To build a weapon for the sky."

"A bridge," Danea said quickly.

"A bridge of flame."

He ignored her.

"Do you know how many harvests failed this winter? How many children slept in cold rooms? How many elders died before they should have because the heat ran thin?" His voice broke, and in the fracture, Sera glimpsed the boy who had brought her twisted nails as if they were treasures. "You called it rationing. You told us it was the sun. All the while you—"

"All the while I planned," Sera said, pain steady as iron. "Because I could not wait for consensus while the sky forgot us. Because faith that does not move the hand is only breath on glass."

Jonar took one step back, as if distance could keep him from the shape of her decision. "You made yourself our god," he whispered.

"No," Sera answered. "I made myself responsible."

Danea reached for him. "Jonar, listen."

He pulled away, palms open, surrender and accusation in the same gesture.

"The Council will hear of this. They must."

"They will," Sera said. "From me. Not from you. And when they rage, I will stand in the flame of their anger and not move."

He laughed again, hoarse, unbelieving. "You will be removed."

"Then remove me," she said, and the heat well brightened with the calm of her resolve. "But you will not remove the capacitors. I buried them in bedrock older than our gods. Try, and you will crack the city."

He stared at her for a long time, and what she saw in his face did not belong to this argument—it belonged to a lifetime of labour and devotion and the ache of loving someone who belonged to more than family. He was her son and her opposition at once.

When he spoke, his voice was quiet and terrible.

"You have betrayed the Thalanor, Mother."

Sera waited.

Let the words pass through her. Felt them settle like slag in a river, heavy and real.

"I have kept us," she said.

"Some of us. It is the only keeping left."

He bowed, too deep, too precise, and left without another word.

Danea sat still. The heat well hissed softly, the sound of an old kettle remembering a boil.

"I will help you," she said.

"Whatever the Council decides. But you must speak to them before Jonar does. Otherwise, they will burn your truth into rumour and call it doctrine."

Sera smiled, a slow curl that held no triumph. "You were always my better teacher."

Danea rose and kissed her mother's brow—the way she had kissed countless foreheads cooling under her fingers.

Then she left, and Sera was alone with the heat.

The Temple of Vessels was hewn around a natural fount where molten crystal welled up from the crust and hardened into clear pillars as tall as towers. The pillars ringed the central dais, refracting the temple's light into wandering spectrums that slid across faces and floors. Today, the spectrum bled redder than gold.

High Priests and Keepers filled the tiers. The city's law was written in their scars and in the way their hands lay flat on their knees—palm to heat, heat to oath. When Sera stepped onto the dais, the murmurs ceased. She set her staff down; its contact with the stone sent a ripple through the floor— recognised authority.

"Brothers. Sisters," she said, voice carrying without effort.

"We have less time than we believed."

She told them everything—the measurements, the graphs, the failing winds. She spoke of the mirrors' code, of Kaedon's dreams, of the map the universe might have left in its own light. She did not speak like a supplicant or a priest; she spoke like an anvil: solid, ringing, impossible to ignore.

And then she confessed.

"I have diverted a portion of the Heart's yield these past cycles," she said.

A movement ran through the chamber—a single inhalation. "That energy sits in sealed capacitors beneath the southern ridge. With Lumera Sael's guidance and Tavir Kelen's ships, with Kaedon Vareth's codes, we will use these stores to prime the Sky Arks and launch four thousand souls, one thousand from each clan-nation, toward the Second Sun."

A priest rose, face flushed to the ears. "You stole fire."

"I husbanded it," Sera returned. "For a winter you have not yet felt."

Another stood, voice sharp. "And left our furnaces wanting? Our harvests thin?"

"I rationed so that there would be something left to ration," she said.

Accusations struck like sparks: treason, blasphemy, hubris. She let them strike. Let them burn out in the open air. When the din broke, she lifted her hand, and the room fell, reflexively, to silence.

"We can choose a perfect death," she said. "All of us together warm to the end. We can call it dignity and stand on the dais and sing while the sky closes its eye. Or we can choose an ugly survival—partial, painful, insufficient—and send our children like embers into a wind we do not control."

She swept her gaze across them, finding old friends and old adversaries, the ones who had held her up after Varen died, the ones who had tried to take her place three times and failed.

"I will choose the ugly thing," she said softly. "Because the beautiful thing is a lie."

The chamber held its breath. It is a hard world that loves truth for itself; harder still when truth demands subtraction.

From the fourth tier, a figure stood—ancient, small, wrapped in a robe embroidered with flames so faded they looked like smoke. Keeper Anesh, who had witnessed Sera's ascension and buried three High Flame Keepers before her. His voice was thin, but when he spoke, the pillars seemed to listen.

"Who will you choose?" he asked. "For the four hundred."

Sera did not hesitate.

"Not those who deserve it most. Not those who can pay. We will choose a seed of what we are: engineers and healers, poets, and pilots, farmers, and midwives. Old and young. Artists. Sceptics. Believers. We will choose the inconvenient and the impossible, the ones the world reshapes itself around. Or we will send a body with no heart into the dark."

"And the rest?" another voice demanded, breaking on the last word.

Sera breathed once, deeply.

"The rest will stand with me. We will keep the fires burning until the last Ark vanishes from the sky. Then we will open the forges and let the heat go back to the earth, and we will sit among the Flame Trees and tell the children what we did and why, and we will wait for the air to grow clear and the night to grow long, and we will sing."

Silence. Then a sound like a sigh moving through stone: acceptance and refusal braided so tightly they became one.

"Bring us the capacitors' schematics," Keeper Anesh said at last. "Bring us proof. Bring us names for the first hundred."

Sera bowed her head. Not victory. Not defeat. A narrow, perilous path between.

She left the temple through a side passage and walked alone beneath the city's skin. The maintenance tunnels here ran close to the surface, and in certain places, the rock thinned to translucent plates where the molten rivers showed like veins. At one such window, she stopped.

On the other side of the glass, the world flowed—a slow, luminous current. She pressed her palm against it and remembered a night long ago when a brazier flame bent toward a mirror and became, for a breath, one thing.

Varen's voice rose in memory, warm and teasing. Arch-Priestess of Stubborn.

"Of hope," she corrected aloud, and smiled.

Her comm-bead clicked softly. A tight whisper filled her ear—half wind, half static. Tavir.

"Flame Keeper," he said, voice pitched low. "Federation patrols have moved south. Someone's talking."

"Of course they are," Sera said. "Hot things make noise."

"Can your capacitors be moved?"

"They can be detonated," she said dryly. "Which is why they'll stay where they are."

"And Jonar?"

"My son believes I have betrayed our people," Sera said. "He may be right."

A pause. The sound of air over metal. "We betray many things to keep the one that matters."

"Then fly, storm-man," she said. "Hide your ships. When the time comes, I will give you a dawn to ride."

She cut the line and stood with her palm against the rock until the heat mapped itself onto the old scars on her hand. Then she turned and walked toward the southern ridge— toward the sealed doors, the sleeping capacitors, the secret she had turned into a choice.

Above her, Ember City rang with hammers and prayers. Beneath her, the planet shifted, restless and mortal.

And in her chest, a flame that others might call faith burned with the stubbornness of a star refusing to die quietly.

CHAPTER 5

Winds of Defiance

The wind had teeth that night. It tore across the upper atmosphere in shrieking spirals, scattering dust, crackling with static. The floating city of Zephara rocked on its tethers, its underside gleaming with sheets of charged light.

To those below, it appeared like a broken halo drifting through storm clouds.

To those who lived upon it, it was home—a city built on courage and air.

In the heart of it stood Tavir Kelen, Chancellor of the Sky Federation, standing on the veranda of his residence and letting the storm lash his face.

He felt alive here.

Grounded people never understood that to the Aerethi, fear and wind were the same thing.

Proof that you were still breathing.

The house behind him sighed with the constant hum of the wind-chamber, the great organ that sang when currents passed through it. It was a family symbol. His father had tuned it by hand; his wife still played it when she was angry.

Tonight, it sounded mournful.

Tavir raised a hand, tasting the air.

The charge was wrong.

The high-altitude currents had thinned again, and that meant less lift for the Sky Arks.

The Arks were his obsession: three completed, four half-built, and eleven dreams in pieces across the wind yards.

If he failed, the last hope of Aurethis would fall with him.

He turned as the door opened.

Nivara, his wife, stepped out, a navigator even now, her hair bound in the practical braids of a pilot. Age had etched silver through her dark-gold skin, but her eyes were still the sharp blue of lightning about to strike.

"You're courting pneumonia," she said, though there was fondness beneath the bite.

He smiled without humour. "Storm's dying. I wanted to feel it."

Nivara moved beside him, her gaze sweeping the horizon where Zephara's other islands drifted in slow procession. "You spoke with the others?"

"I did." He rested his forearms on the rail, knuckles whitening.

"The sun's going. Faster than we thought."

Nivara didn't flinch; she had flown through lightning for half her life. "And your friends?"

"Lumera believes she's found a path to a second sun.

Sera's prepared to burn her world to light ours.

"Kaedon…" He hesitated, hearing the faint echo of the Varethine's calm voice. "Kaedon believes in stories. I think that might be what saves us."

"And you?" she asked.

"I believe in motion," Tavir said.

"If we stay still, we're already dead."

Later, in the council hall, a vast amphitheatre built from storm glass, Tavir faced the Federation's High Council. They sat in a crescent of gleaming chairs that arced like a wing around the chamber, their robes fluttering faintly in the draft from the open dome above.

The storm's low growl filtered in, a sound like breathing.

"Chancellor Kelen," said Admiral Serrin, the eldest among them, "you were summoned to explain why half of Zephara's fuel reserves have gone missing."

Tavir clasped his hands behind his back.

"They haven't gone missing. They've been reallocated."

"Reallocated," Serrin repeated, the word sour. "To where?"

"The Sky Arks."

A murmur rippled through the council, wings of disapproval beating softly in the half-light.

Serrin leaned forward.

"You have no authorization. The Arks were decommissioned. The Federation agreed the project was—"

"Impractical," Tavir finished for him.

"Yes. Because we chose comfort over courage."

The admiral's face hardened.

"Mind your tone."

"I'm running out of time to mind anything," Tavir said.

He touched the control band on his wrist, and the air between them shimmered, projecting a holographic map of the star's decaying field.

"The sun is dying. Within months, the upper ion streams will collapse. When that happens, Zephara will fall. The Arks are our only way to leave orbit before the currents vanish."

Serrin's voice turned icy.

"And where exactly would we go? You intend to fly into the void on the whim of a Solenari myth?"

"Not a myth," Tavir said. "A trajectory. Lumera Sael has found the coordinates. Kaedon Vareth has the codes to interpret them."

"Philosophers," Serrin spat. "And dreamers."

"And builders," Tavir said. "We need all three if we want to exist long enough to argue about it."

A younger councillor, Veyra Rin, rose halfway from her seat. "Even if this... Illumeris exists, you can't take everyone."

"No," Tavir said. "But we can take enough to begin again."

"And who chooses who lives and who dies?" Serrin's voice cracked like a whip. "You?"

Tavir met his gaze. "Someone must. Or no one will."

The council erupted.

Voices rising like a storm, echoing against glass and thunder.

Words like treason and madness flew as freely as sparks. Tavir stood still, letting it wash over him. He had expected resistance; fear always dressed itself in righteousness.

When silence finally returned, Serrin said softly, "You're dismissed. And as of now, you are relieved of command."

Tavir gave a single, curt nod. "Then I am free to act."

He turned and walked out before they could order his arrest.

Outside, the wind howled, but Tavir felt calm.

He crossed the suspension bridge to his private hangar; its edges rimed with blue lightning. Inside, engineers paused at his arrival.

Many had served him for decades; they knew that expression—the one that meant we are about to do something unforgivable.

"Captain Ryn Kelen!" Tavir's voice cut through the clamour.

From beneath the belly of a half-built Ark, a tall, broad-shouldered man emerged—his son.

Ryn wiped grease from his hands, his face smeared with the metallic soot of the hangar.

His resemblance to Tavir was uncanny, save for the darker edge in his gaze. They had not spoken civilly for months.

"You're not supposed to be here," Ryn said. "The Council suspended your access."

"Then you'd better look surprised when the alarms go off," Tavir said.

"I'm taking the Veyra."

"That ship isn't flight-certified," Ryn said sharply. "Its stabilisers are untested, and half the storm shielding is patched from spare hulls."

"Perfect," Tavir said. "It'll feel like home."

"Father," Ryn said, wiping his palms on his flight vest, "this isn't about engineering—it's about extinction. You think you can save four thousand souls, and then what? Leave the rest of us to choke on ashes?"

Tavir's voice softened. "If we stay, none of us will have air to choke on."

"And if you fail?"

"Then at least the sky will remember we tried."

Ryn shook his head slowly.

"You always talked about courage, but I think you mean guilt. You're trying to out-fly your own."

Tavir flinched, not from anger but from the precision of the wound.

"I lost your brother to a faulty stabiliser. I won't lose the species to hesitation."

Silence stretched between them, heavy as gravity. Then Ryn said quietly, "You'll need a pilot."

"I already have one," Tavir said, but his son was already walking toward the ladder.

"Good," Ryn said. "Because I'm taking her up with or without you."

The hangar doors opened onto a storm-black sky.

Wind rushed in, carrying the scent of ozone and promise. The Sky Ark Veyra hovered on its magnetic tethers, hull gleaming like a storm cloud forged into metal. Lightning crawled across its wings, caught and redirected through its charge conduits.

Nivara appeared at the hatch, hands on her hips, hair whipping in the wind. "You both look ridiculous," she shouted over the roar. "Do it quickly, before someone remembers to arrest you."

Tavir smiled, heart aching with love and defiance. "That's my navigator."

"And your conscience," she said. "Try not to crash into either."

They launched as the alarms began to wail.

The Ark rose through clouds bruised purple and gold, cutting across lightning veins that split the air like rivers of glass. Instruments shrieked warnings; stabilisers groaned under the charge differential. Ryn kept the nose steady, his hands sure on the controls. Tavir manned the storm flares, each pulse a bright defiance against gravity.

At forty thousand spans, the sky turned thin and electric. The surface of Aurethis stretched below them, glimmering like a dying ember. From up here, they could see the fractures spreading across continents—lines of light where molten rivers met cracking crust.

Ryn whispered, "It's beautiful."

"It's dying," Tavir said. "Beauty and death have always shared a colour."

The instruments pinged: a signal, weak but clear, originating from the southern hemisphere. Tavir leaned over the console. "That's Sera. She's sending the new frequency alignment."

"She did it," Ryn said softly.

"Yes," Tavir replied. "She always does."

He looked out at the horizon, where dawn struggled against the dark.

The wind beyond the ship shimmered faintly, and for an instant, Tavir imagined he saw two suns reflected in the clouds.

The dying one behind him, and its phantom twin ahead.

Hours later, when they returned to Zephara, Federation enforcers were waiting. The docks blazed with searchlights; the Council's insignia flickered across the comms network. Tavir's crew scattered before the order could be given. Ryn shut down the engines and leaned back in his seat, chest heaving.

"Well," he said, "that went better than expected."

"Always does," Tavir said.

Outside, the arresting officers shouted commands. Tavir turned to his son and grinned, lightning flashing in his teeth. "You can still leave. Tell them you tried to stop me."

Ryn shook his head. "I think I'd rather fly."

They stepped out together, side by side, as the storm broke over Zephara. Rain hissed on the hull, washing away the residue of the sky.

When they were taken into custody, Tavir did not resist. He looked upward through the translucent dome of the city, toward the faint golden scar where the sun bled through clouds.

Even from here, it looked smaller.

He smiled, not with peace, but with resolve.

They could chain his hands, but they could not still the wind.

And somewhere beneath the crust, Sera Thal's forges waited to burn.

CHAPTER 6

The Mirror Code

The descent into Thrayne was like entering the memory of the world. Kaedon Vareth stepped from the ore-lift into the cool breath of the caverns and closed his eyes. The air here carried a damp mineral sweetness, the scent of stone that had learned to hold history. Aboveground, the sky screamed and scorched; below, the planet whispered.

He had always trusted whispers.

Light-fungi brightened at his presence, a soft blue shimmer sensate as dew.

The tunnel widened to the Obsidian Archive, and the chamber revealed itself in layered echoes—a cathedral carved from glass and night. Pillars of volcanic glass rose like frozen smoke; their surfaces engraved with spirals of script that shone when sung to. Pools nested in terraces reflected blue starlight that wasn't there, only the patient glow of life below the ground.

Evara waited in the entryway, robed in slate and silver.

Her hands bore the fine grit of a sculptor; her eyes, the steadiness of a keeper of truth.

"You walk like the sky broke your bones," she said gently.

"It broke my schedule," Kaedon replied, smiling.

"The bones were already brittle."

She touched his cheek, with the tenderness of a long companionship that had outlasted passion and grown into shelter.

"You missed the evening pulse. The fungi were murmuring of change."

"They're not wrong." He handed her the travel wrap. "Call Lynis. And Neriel if the Choir is at rest. We have work to wake up for."

Evara's brow lifted. "The Four?"

"The Four," he said, and the word filled the Archive like a chord: light, shadow, wind, flame—returning to one another's gravity.

Lynis came first, guided by her long staff tipped with a sliver of mirror-stone. Blindness had not diminished her certainty; if anything, it honed it.

The glow beneath her skin pulsed brighter than Kaedon remembered, a clear river of light moving through darkness.

"You smell like ozone," she said, her laugh a feathered thing. "Tavir left the wind tangled in your cloak."

"And Lumera left equations in my pockets."

Kaedon touched the satchel on his hip.

"Sera left a taste of iron in my mouth. We carry our friends like elements."

Lynis lifted her face as if to drink the air. "And the sun?"

"Smaller, and nearer," he said. "How can it be both?"

She did not answer, but the quiet between them agreed.

Neriel arrived with Sira and their boy, Darel, trailing—and suddenly Kaedon felt the pressure of time not as a cosmic thing but as an ordinary hunger.

Neriel, all gentle scholarship, and weary loyalty.

Sira, smelling faintly of moss and saline, as if she carried gardens in her sleeves.

Darel, fourteen cycles, eyes bright with forbidden sunlight, that rare Varethine hunger to stand in something that burned.

"Grandfather," Darel blurted before Neriel could scold him for interrupting, "did you see the mirror fields? Did they sing? Is it true the sky has two hearts?"

Neriel raised a palm. "Darel."

"Let him ask," Kaedon said. "He is asking well."

He considered and then responded.

"The mirrors trembled. The wind sang the wrong song. And yes, if you know how to listen, you can hear a second beat behind the sun."

Darel's breath caught.

Sira placed a hand on the boy's shoulder, a tether of love.

"We're with you," Neriel said softly. "Whatever this becomes."

Kaedon nodded. "Then we begin."

The Dream Well lay in the Archive's heart: a circular pit where water slept in a polished bowl of obsidian, its surface perfectly still.

Above it, suspended by six braided cables of storm glass, hung the Harmonic Frame, an instrument of tuning forks and chimes that translated sung tone into vibration in stone. For centuries, the Varethine had used it to carve thought into mirror.

Tonight, Kaedon would ask it to carve a path into the dark.

He placed Lumera's triangular shard on a low plinth by the well.

It pulsed faintly, as if catching breath. Across from it, he set the Mirror Code, the obsidian slab inscribed with sigils that had outlived empires. Between them, a narrow span of air glittered with dust motes and possibility.

"Evara," he said, "the spindle."

She opened a velvet case and drew out a thin crystal, a song spindle, scored with minute grooves.

"The oldest resonance on record," she said. "Taken from the first echo of the planet after the Convergence. It listens longer than we can."

Kaedon lifted the spindle to his ear out of old habit, as if it were a seashell and a memory both. Then he fitted it into the Frame's cradle.

"Lynis," he said.

She stepped forward, staff touching the floor with the certainty of a metronome.

"You will want F-major to wake the slab, A-minor to ask it to speak, then the interval of a tritone to make it disagree with itself."

"To disagree. Why?"

"So, it will admit it knows more than it is saying." Lynis smiled.

"Truth is a shy animal. Contradiction makes it bold."

"Of course it does," Kaedon murmured, delighted. "Darel. Watch."

The boy took a position at his elbow, vibrating with concentration.

Kaedon inhaled and let the Archive come through him.

He sang beautifully and with precision.

The first tone trembled the floor; the second drew a low responding hum from the obsidian. The third, Lynis's dissonant knife, split the air.

The fungus dimmed as if holding breath.

The Dream Well's water quivered, then stilled, and a thin line of light leapt from the shard to the slab.

It was so small at first, just a thread, but in it lived a language that was not words: a syntax of flicker and pause, bright and dim, like a heartbeat describing a map.

"There you are," Kaedon whispered. "Come then. Say your name."

He adjusted the forks one by one; fingers gentle as in prayer.

The line thickened.

Symbols bloomed between shard and slab, faint as fog: spirals nested in spirals, two interlocking coils that made both an eye and a path.

Darel gasped. "Twin suns!"

"Not suns." Lynis tilted her head, listening with the bones.

"Two throats. One breath."

The light stuttered and went out.

Kaedon swallowed, steadied his voice.

"Again."

They tuned, sang, tuned again.

Hours fell like leaves.

The line returned, faltered, returned stronger. Evara changed the temperature in the room by opening and closing vents—heat and cool meant different arguments to glass.

At last, the space between shard and slab filled with a translucent helix, turning slowly. Points along it brightened, then dimmed in a sequence—not random.

Waymarks.

"Record," Kaedon said, and Neriel's fingers flew, capturing the sequence on a slate. Sira sketched the helix's proportions, her botanist's hand precise as root and vein.

"What are they?" Darel asked, voice trembling.

"Positions," Kaedon said. His mouth was dry.

"Windows where the river between stars runs nearest to us. Corridors where light is easiest to follow."

"Stellar currents," Neriel breathed. "Refractive channels."

"Sky rivers," Darel whispered, and in his voice, Kaedon heard the Aerethi word, learned from contraband songs.

The helix shimmered with a second pattern, a faint counterpoint, not light but shadow, a negative of illumination. Where one brightened, the other nearly vanished; where one dimmed, the second swelled.

"Resonant refusal. The map and the room it does not wish to enter," Lynis said softly.

Kaedon adjusted the tritone by a fraction.

The two patterns slid over one another and, for a heartbeat, aligned.

When they did, the Dream Well's water flashed white, and an image rose from its surface: a star field not of Aurethis, but of a sky Kaedon had never seen. Far away, a young gold brightened. Around it, a dim blue-green pearl.

Evara's breath broke.

Sira's hand found Neriel's.

Darel took one step toward the water, then stopped, reverent.

Kaedon did not move at all. He had waited his whole life for a silence this loud.

"Is that...?" Darel's voice was a thread.

"An answer," Kaedon said. "Not a promise. A door, not a destination."

The image flickered. The helix wavered. The Frame sang wrong.

"Hold it," Kaedon said through his teeth. "Just once more—hold—"

Pain lanced through his skull.

Not sound exactly, pressure, as if something very large had leaned down to hear him better and mistaken his head for the floor. He gripped the rail. The helix thinned. He felt the Archive strain with him; the pillars groaned softly. The Dream Well's water dimpled.

Lynis moved, swift and surely. She lifted her staff and struck the floor once, hard.

The sound that followed was not a note.

It was a stop.

A clean subtraction that cut the pressure in halves and thirds until the room remembered itself.

The image vanished.

The helix retracted and then dissolved. Only the shard and the slab remained, pulsing faintly as if embarrassed by what they'd revealed.

Kaedon sagged into Evara's hands. She steadied him with a quiet murmur. His breath returned one length at a time.

"Enough," she said. "You're not a boy."

"I was for a moment," he said, laughing breathlessly. "And the universe noticed."

Lynis crouched, head tilted. "You were leaning too hard," she said, amused and kind. "Truth will be courted, not cornered."

"We saw it," Darel insisted, face alight with raw holiness. "We saw it!"

Kaedon reached for him and gripped his shoulder.

"Yes, child. We did."

Neriel pressed a cool cloth to Kaedon's forehead.

"Can you do it again?"

"Yes," Kaedon said. "But not now."

He closed his eyes.

"Now we preserve what we have and write the next step at a pace that won't break us."

He gestured, and Sira brought the slates.

Together they reviewed the sequence twice, three times, until the shapes wrote themselves on the back of Kaedon's eyelids.

He heard the pattern as a melody and hummed it under his breath. The Archive hummed with him, pleased by good work.

Evara poured tea with the ceremonial patience of a sculptor finishing a curve. They drank in silence, letting their pulses slow to the room's old rhythm.

Only then did the outside world arrive.

Footsteps at the threshold—soft and many.

Kaedon turned to see three Council Scribes in grey, faces arranged in neutrality. Behind them stood Archivist Jorel, a man Kaedon had mentored and then disagreed with for forty years.

"Dream-Scribe Vareth," Jorel said, and then he bowed exactly to the degree of courtesy required and no more.

"The Council requests a record of tonight's research and an account of Lumera Sael's visit."

"We have already made a record," Kaedon said pleasantly. "As is our habit. You may have a copy at dawn."

"We will take it now," Jorel said, eyes sliding toward the shard with a hunger he thought he'd hidden.

"For safekeeping."

Evara shifted to put herself between the plinth and Jorel, a small domestic motion that in her hands became a line drawn across a continent.

"For safekeeping," she repeated mildly, "in the same vault you gave to the zealots who cracked three thought-stones trying too 'clean' them?"

Colour rose to Jorel's cheeks.

"National secrets are not debating fodder."

Kaedon smiled. "No. They are songs. And I am not done composing."

Lynis tapped her staff once.

The light-fungi along the walls dimmed, then rose.

The Archive's acoustics changed subtly, a cue the Scribes did not know, but every Varethine child did: you are a guest here, not a master.

"We will deliver a copy at dawn," Kaedon repeated, softer.

"And I will deliver a second copy personally to the Equinox Crossroads."

He met Jorel's gaze.

"The Golden Accord stands, whether or not your fear does."

Jorel's mouth tightened. He was not a cruel man, only a careful one.

Care could harden until it cracked.

"Be prudent, Kaedon. You are old."

"I am precise," Kaedon said. "It looks similar from a distance."

The Scribes withdrew with stiff bows.

When their steps faded, the Archive relaxed audibly—the stones released a breath.

Neriel exhaled. "They'll be back with guards."

"Yes," Kaedon said. "Which means we will not be here."

"Where?" Sira asked.

He looked toward the lower tunnels—the old routes Varethine used when they wished to be both present and gone.

"To the outfalls. The Shadow Walkers there owe me favours and hate Council boots. We will copy the sequence and carry it in three ways: as light on crystal, as tone in stone, and as story in the mouth."

Darel's eyes shone. "Can I carry the story?"

"Not yet," Neriel said automatically.

"Yes," Kaedon said and smiled at his son's look of alarm.

"Because he will not carry it alone."

He turned to Lynis.

"You heard more than I did."

"I always do," she said lightly.

"Will you sing it with him?"

She inclined her head.

"We will teach the cadence to the boy. If the crystals shatter and the stones refuse, the words will find each other again across mouths."

Evara touched Kaedon's wrist. "And you?"

"I will go up," he said. "There is a place near the surface where a blade of light falls at noon through a crack in the rock. If the helix is what I believe that blade will strike a different facet today."

"Dangerous," she said.

"And necessarily," he answered. "Tavir will need a lattice to fly. Lumera will need a key to keep the sequence stable under acceleration. Sera will need a pulse count to prime her capacitors. I can give them these—if I find one more note."

He took Lumera's shard, wrapped it in dark cloth, and slipped it inside his tunic. It throbbed faintly against his ribs, like a second heart that preferred mathematics to blood.

He kissed Evara's brow, then Lynis's.

He squeezed Neriel's shoulder, then rested his palm on Darel's head, blessing, and apology in one touch.

"Eat," he told them.

"Pack lightly. Tell no one you don't trust. At dawn-tenth, go to the south outfalls and whisper my name to the rock. It will open."

"What will you do if the Council intercepts you before then?" Neriel asked.

"Tell them a story," Kaedon said. "And ask them if they remember how to listen."

He left through a maintenance shaft and climbed toward the thin seam where the world leaked light. The path knew his feet; he had walked it as a young scribe, when he still believed all arguments could be won with grace. He walked it now as an old one, who knew some arguments must be endured like weather.

At the fissure, noon cut the dark—just as he'd hoped.

A blade of sun slid down the wall, struck a patch of mineral barely larger than his palm, and scattered itself into a miniature constellation on the opposite face. He angled the shard into the beam. The light took the gift greedily and poured through it. Symbols skittered across the stone like startled fish, then settled into an array.

He sang the tritone softer this time. Asked, not demanded. The array rotated once.

"Say your name," he whispered.

It did not. Instead, it offered a rhythm. Three bright pulses, a pause, two dim, a longer silence, then five, repeating, then reversing.

A network of time.

"Launch window," Kaedon murmured.

"And a refusal window. A sky that opens and then snaps shut."

He wrote it in his bones by repeating it under his breath. He etched it onto the shard by laying the crystal against the warm stone. He snapped a sliver from his own staff and carved the rhythm into it with his thumbnail, bleeding a little because he believed the universe paid attention to gifts that cost something.

When he was done, he sat with his back to the rock and let the weak noon sun warm his face. He thought of Lumera's tower, Tavir's storm, Sera's fire, and felt the strange grace of being the shadow among such brightness. Stories did not need light to grow; they needed truth and someone stubborn enough to carry them.

Footsteps approached along the seam. He did not turn. He knew the cadence.

"Archivist Jorel," he said, before the other man could marshal an expression. "You walk loudly for a careful man."

"I came alone," Jorel said, voice tight.

"You are forcing my hand."

"I am freeing it," Kaedon said mildly.

"You have spent your life clinging to rules because you were afraid your heart would fall. Let it."

Jorel hesitated. "If you're wrong, you damn us."

"If I am wrong," Kaedon said, "we are damned already. If I am right, you may live long enough to scold me in a new sky."

The other man made a small, ragged sound that might have been a laugh if it weren't so close to sobbing.

"What did you see?" Jorel asked, stripped at last of pretence. He wasn't a monster; he was a man who wanted to be certain. Certainty had become a luxury the world could no longer afford.

Kaedon lifted the shard toward the narrow sun. "I saw a door," he said. "And beyond it, a room that will remember us if we learn how to enter politely."

Jorel closed his eyes.

"Take the southern outfalls."

He pressed something into Kaedon's hand.

An old key, its grooves worn smooth by generations.

"They watch the eastern vents. I will misfile your record for a day."

"Thank you," Kaedon said simply.

"Don't thank me," Jorel muttered. "Bring my grandchildren a sky."

Kaedon tucked the key away, then rose. His knees complained; he praised them anyway.

On the walk back to the Archive, the fungus along the walls pulsed in a sequence he now recognised: three bright, pause, two dim, long silence, five. He laughed aloud, a sound that bounced off the glass and returned richer.

"I hear you," he told the stone. "We're coming as fast as our old feet will carry us."

At the Archive door, Darel waited, a pack on his shoulders too large for his frame, a grin too large for his face.

"Teach me the cadence," the boy demanded.

Kaedon did and made him repeat it until his tongue and lungs had agreed. Then he took Neriel's slate, Sira's sketch roll, Lynis's staff-tip, and Evara's spindle case, and bound them with a strap stamped with the sigil burned into Lumera's floor: two interlocking spirals.

When the binding was done, he felt the weight of it—not the objects, but what they implied.

Proof.

Not enough to erase doubt, but enough to make it ashamed of itself.

He sent a quick pulse along the whisper-line to Lumera's tower, Tavir's hangar, Sera's temple—a courier note in tones only their instruments would recognise.

WE HAVE A DOOR.

WINDOW THREE—PAUSE—TWO—LONG— FIVE.

CARRY STORY AS BACKUP.

PREPARE.

He touched his forehead to the cool obsidian of the entryway and spoke the simplest prayer he knew, which was not a request, but a promise.

"I will tell the truth the way the world tells it," he said. "In echoes. Patiently. Until someone hears."

Then Kaedon Vareth, Dream-Scribe Laureate of the caverns, stepped into the tunnels leading toward the south outfalls.

Toward secrecy, toward danger, toward the uncertain grace of being necessary—and the Archive dimmed its light politely behind him.

CHAPTER 7

The Fractured Light

The news reached Lumera Sael through the mirrors. Not through messengers, not through couriers, but through the very lattice of light that webbed across the Solenari plateaus—a whisper that travelled by reflection, faster than any word.

At first, it was only a flicker, a change in rhythm. Then it became unmistakable: the coded pulse Kaedon had promised her.

Three bright, pause, two dim, long silence, five.

She was in her study atop the Glass Tower when it came.

The room was still; the instruments resting in their crystalline hum, the air dry and metallic from weeks of failing sunlight. Taren, her husband, was pruning the heliotrope vines on the balcony. She almost called to him, almost, but didn't.

This moment was for her alone.

"We have a door," she whispered, repeating the message as if the act itself might make it truer. "A door through the dark."

The mirrors responded in a trembling chorus.

Deep within their frequency, she imagined she heard Kaedon's voice—patient, weary, certain.

He had found it.

The path.

The coordinates were real.

And yet the timing of his message carried another meaning.

It was not only a discovery—it was a warning.

The laboratories of Aurion's Edge pulsed with uneasy light.

Rows of mirrored spires rose like frozen lightning across the plateau, each a beacon feeding into the planetary network.

Inside, scientists in copper-threaded robes worked in near silence. Gone was the chatter of optimism that had once filled these halls; the hum of the machinery had taken on a hollow resonance, as if the world itself had grown cautious of sound.

Lumera descended into the central forge—her domain.

The air shimmered with heat ghosts, though the temperature had dropped sharply in recent months. She placed her palm on the main prism-core, and the glass beneath her hand came alive, flooding the chamber with light.

Her chief engineer, Aurek Sael, entered moments later, his face flushed from haste. Her son had inherited her intellect but not her reverence; where she saw wonder, he saw engineering problems.

"Mother," he said, voice clipped, "the Mirror Fields are weakening again. Two stations went dark overnight. We can't keep the grid aligned without more power from the Ember trade lines."

"We'll have no more shipments from Dravonar," Lumera replied.

"Sera is preparing her final ignition."

Aurek's eyes hardened.

"So, the rumours are true."

"She's doing what she must."

"She's burning what she mustn't."

He ran a hand through his short-cropped silver hair, a nervous habit.

"You're all chasing myths. Sera's forges, Tavir's Arks, your maps in the sun. Even the Varethine are singing prophecies again. It's all madness."

Lumera turned from him, adjusting the prism's focus until the light narrowed into a column sharp enough to cast their reflections against the far wall.

"You were a child the last time the sun flared strong," she said softly. "You don't remember what the world used to be. None of your generation does. But you will remember what we tried."

"Trying doesn't save anyone," he snapped.

"No," she said, and faced him fully. "But surrender saves no one at all."

Aurek's anger flickered, briefly replaced by something like fear. "What happens if your 'door' opens onto nothing?"

"Then we die," Lumera said.

"But not blind."

By nightfall, the wind had turned harsh again.

Dust from the dying plains drifted upward, dimming the once-clear mirrors. Lumera returned to the tower's top chamber, the observatory that looked directly into the heart of the sun.

Taren was waiting for her there, leaning against the balcony rail. The fading light painted him in honeyed bronze, softening the lines age had carved. He smiled when she approached.

"You've been with the light again," he said. "I could see it dancing across the glass from the gardens."

"Kaedon found something," she said.

"A resonance. Proof of Illumeris."

He raised an eyebrow.

"The Second Sun."

"The very one."

Taren's smile faded into the quiet sadness of a man who loved both his wife and her obsessions. "And now you'll go chasing it."

"I have to."

He looked past her, toward the horizon where the dying star pulsed faintly like a wounded heart.

"Do you ever think," he said, "that we might have been meant to end here? That perhaps every world has a lifespan, and trying to outlive it is a kind of theft?"

Lumera moved to stand beside him. "Then let us be thieves, love. Thieves of time, of light, of memory. Let us steal one more dawn."

They stood together as the wind howled around the tower, the mirrors below shivering in sympathy.

The following morning, the Council of the Lumen Mothers convened in the Hall of Refracted Truths.

Seven elder women sat in a semicircle before her, each face luminous in the filtered light of the high mirrors.

The youngest among them, Mother Veira, spoke first.

"High Engineer Sael," she began, voice measured, "you stand accused of diverting mirror energy to unauthorised transmissions—of sharing Solenari secrets with foreign nations. Do you deny this?"

Lumera bowed her head slightly. "I do not."

A murmur passed among the Mothers.

Veira's expression faltered; she had expected denial.

Mother Eryel, the eldest, leaned forward.

"And why should we not interpret that as treason?"

"Because what I share is not weaponry but hope," Lumera said evenly. "A map to survival."

"Hope is not our jurisdiction," another Mother said sharply.

"Order is. The Solenari endure because we guard the light—not scatter it to the winds."

"And what will you guard?" Lumera asked, "when there is no light left?"

The room fell silent.

It was Eryel who spoke again, voice softer.

"The Council cannot sanction your project. The Mirror Temples must conserve what power remains to sustain the people. We will not waste it chasing ghosts."

"Then I will chase them alone," Lumera said.

"But I will not stand idle while the world fades."

Eryel's gaze softened.

"Lumera, you were once our brightest mirror. Do not become a fracture."

Lumera smiled faintly. "Even a fracture lets the light through."

She left the hall to the sound of their low arguments echoing in her wake.

Back in her private chambers, Lumera activated the hidden frequency link Kaedon had designed decades ago—a sliver of light encoded to bend only toward the right mirrors.

It pulsed once, connecting the remaining three members of the Golden Accord.

Tavir's face appeared first, windblown, and defiant.

Sera followed, her skin glowing with forge-light.

Kaedon's came last, shadowed by stone.

"You received it," Kaedon said. His voice carried the tired joy of victory snatched from the brink.

"I did," Lumera replied. "And I've been excommunicated for believing you."

Tavir grinned. "Welcome to the club."

"The Council knows?" Sera asked.

"They know enough," Lumera said. "I'll be stripped of title by dawn."

"Then we move before dawn," Tavir said.

"Zephara's under martial orders. I've only a few hours before they ground every Ark."

Kaedon inclined his head.

"The coordinates are encoded in both shadow and light. You'll each need a harmonic converter to translate your local frequencies. Lumera, do you still have access to the central prism forge?"

"Until sunrise," she said.

"Then forge three converters—one for each of us. I'll send the alignment tones through the mirror grid."

"And the launch window?" Sera asked.

Kaedon's image flickered; his voice came in waves.

"Three—pause—two—long—five. That's the cycle. You must ignite at the third flare interval. If you miss it..."

"Then the door closes," Tavir finished.

Sera's eyes narrowed. "And how long until that first window?"

Kaedon's pause was heavy.

"Six weeks."

Lumera exhaled, every calculation in her mind whirring to life.

Six weeks to align the mirrors, recalibrate the solar crucibles, and deliver converters to the others.

Six weeks before Aurethis lost its last chance.

"Then we begin," she said.

Tavir's grin softened.

"You always make damnation sound like duty."

"Because it is," Lumera said.

The link dissolved, their images scattering back into the fractured light.

That night, Lumera worked alone. The tower glowed like a beacon against the dying horizon, each floor pulsing with activity. From afar, it must have looked as if the sun had taken refuge in one last citadel before surrendering to dark.

She stood before the forge at the tower's heart, the Mirror Crucible, a great sphere of tempered glass that harnessed the focused light of a hundred mirrors. She stripped away her ceremonial robes and donned a heat-resistant mantle of copper thread. Her fingers moved with the precision of devotion.

Each converter she forged was a marriage of science and prayer—a device capable of translating Kaedon's harmonic code into navigational data.

The first she named Wind's Promise, for Tavir.

The second, Flame's Oath, for Sera.

The third she kept nameless, to be delivered into whatever future still had room for names.

Hours blurred.

The light shifted from gold to white to blue.

By the time she quenched the final crystal, dawn had touched the edges of the world. She watched the first pale rays climb the horizon and realised how faint they had become.

Taren appeared at the doorway, hair unbound, eyes heavy with sleep.

"You'll kill yourself with this," he said.

"Then I'll die on purpose," she replied.

He crossed the room, took her soot-stained hand, and held it tight.

"At least let me die beside you."

Lumera looked at him, her heart catching in its old, familiar ache.

"No," she whispered. "Someone has to tell them what we did."

She kissed his brow, and the moment stretched.

Fragile as glass, radiant as memory.

Outside, the dying sun flared once, throwing their shadows long across the room. For an instant, their silhouettes merged—one light, two souls.

And deep beneath the earth, in Kaedon's cavern, the harmonic tone of the Mirror Code pulsed again.

The door was opening.

CHAPTER 8

Ashes and Skyfire

By noon, the city burned with rumours. Whispers ignited in alleys, raced along gantries, curled like smoke through the Temple of Vessels, and rose into the sky lanes over Ember City.

The words were always the same, only the flavour changed: Sera stole the heat.

The High Flame Keeper built a secret fire for the sky and left our hearths to starve. There will be no winter if there is no world.

Sera Thal walked through it like a woman crossing her own funeral pyre.

She had dressed without ornament: soot-black mantle, tempered glass bracers, hair bound tight. The heat well in her chamber hummed a steady lower register, as if the city tuned itself to her pulse. Outside, couriers sprinted, bells tolled, three long peals, a pause, two short, a silence, then five: the cadence Kaedon had sent, already turned by rumour into an omen. Thalanor learned fast when fire taught the lesson.

On the landing outside her door, Danea waited with a slate in her arms and a physician's calm at war with a daughter's fear. "The Council meets again in an hour," she said, "and the courtyard is full. They want answers, Mother, not equations."

"They'll have both," Sera replied.

Danea fell in step as Sera descended the spiral steps. "There were scuffles near the western forges at dawn—on the ration lines. We've doubled clinic capacity, but I'll need more glow salt if we keep treating burn-faint."

"Send to the north kilns," Sera said. "Take my name. If they refuse you, take my seal." She tapped the ring on her finger; the sigil of the Flame Keeper ground into glass-metal. "If they still refuse..."

"I'll bring you the names," Danea finished.

She glanced sideways. "Any word from Jonar?"

Heat and ache rose together in Sera's throat.

"He'll come. Men of iron always bend before they break."

"And if he breaks?"

"Then I will hold the pieces until the fire makes him soft again."

They exited onto a balcony overlooking the city.

Ember City unfurled below, tiers of workshops and dwellings surrounding the central Heart of Ember, its domed housings venting plumes that painted the sky with amber steam.

Between rooftops, Flame Trees glowed like constellations pinned to earth; their roots flickered with the slow memories of the dead. Sera touched the rail and felt through glass and grit, the planet's patient heat.

"Six weeks," she murmured. "We must turn a temple into a launch-engine and keep a people alive while we do it."

Danea squeezed her mother's arm. "Then let us begin with names."

The Temple of Vessels had never been so crowded.

A thousand eyes smouldered in the tiers, a thousand palms warmed stone. When Sera stepped onto the central dais, the murmurs fell by habit of silence.

Keeper Anesh rose—ancient, ash-pale, robe embroidered with flames so faint they were mostly memory. "Flame Keeper," he said, voice thin but carrying, "the city asks for reckoning."

Sera bowed, not deeply, respect measured by truth.

"You'll have it."

She faced the crowd.

Not all were Thalanor; there were Solenari traders, Varethine shadow-walkers hugging the columns, two Aerethi pilots perched like patient hawks on the upper rail. It made Sera oddly glad; a city should be many if it hopes to live in more than one sky.

"You've heard the rumours," she said. "I'll make them plain."

She told them everything: the collapse of the sun, the three-two-long-five cycles, the door Kaedon had wrested from shadow and song, the converters Lumera was forging, the Sky Arks Tavir had stolen back from cowardice and law.

She confessed again the diverted heat, the sleeping capacitors beneath the southern ridge, the catapult array she had been building in secret for two decades, shaping blasphemy into possibility.

"Four thousand will fly," she said softly, and the words moved through the chamber like a wind that remembered fire. "A thousand of ours among them. Not the richest. Not the loudest. A seed of us. Healers and engineers, welders, and weavers, glass wrights, midwives, singers of the long work. Children. Elders. Doubters. Believers. We will be many enough to be honest when we tell a new world who we are."

From the second tier, a woman stood, cheeks streaked with ash, mouth a riven coal. "And the rest of us?"

Sera didn't adorn the answer.

"We will keep the forges breathing until the last Ark catches the window. We will open the heat wells and give warmth to the ground, so it holds our dead the way it has always held us. We will tell the children stories that are true. And then, when the long night comes, we will be together."

A murmur, low, and mortal, moved through the tiers.

Not agreement.

Not rejection.

The sound people make when the world shifts inside their ribs and cannot be returned to where it sat.

Keeper Anesh struck the floor with his staff, a sound like a lid settling on a pot. "Bring us your first names."

Danea stepped forward with her slate.

Sera read, and each name felt like lifting a stone that had slept in a river: weight, smoothness, history.

"Sahan Ver," she began, "line-captain of the south quench. Kelri Morn, glass-metal smith, builder of fracture-housings. Iri Vel—a midwife whose hands have warmed a thousand first breaths. Tamal Riv, whose welds have never cracked and whose jokes have always been worse than they should be."

Laughter, thin and grateful, ran across the tiers.

It steadied Sera more than any prayer.

She kept reading: healers and hone-stone carvers, an old woman who remembered the last full Convergence, a boy with hands made for knots and eyes made for measuring wind.

"And Eris Thal," Sera said, voice dipping.

A hush, then a hot wave of whispers.

Danea's head snapped up. "Mother?"

Sera lifted her chin.

"Yes. My granddaughter. Runaway to the Aerethi. She knows the winds better than any in this city and the stubbornness better than any in our family. If she stands for the test, she stands."

A Keeper rose, lips thin. "Favouritism."

"Function," Sera said.

"We will not build an Ark contingent without a person who speaks the sky's grammar."

"Eris isn't here," Danea murmured.

"She will be," Sera said, though she had no right to certainty.

She had only a lifetime of knowing how heat finds its level.

They took twenty more names before the first interruption hit.

The explosion wasn't large. It wasn't meant to be. It was a fist.

The sudden, ugly punctuation of a sentence spoken by those who believed noise made truth.

It came from the western ventilation gallery.

The chamber jolted; dust fell from the pillars like a small, surprised snowfall. Then the alarm bells rang, four quick strikes, a long roll: breach containment, western quarter.

Sera was already moving.

"Danea—triage to the west. Anesh—lock the lower doors. No one in or out without my seal."

She ran the galleries at a pace that should have broken a woman her age and did not. Heat rose in waves from the floor; the air tasted of copper and haste. When she reached the outer corridor, the smell of burnt resin struck her hard enough to salt her eyes.

Two guards knelt by a damaged hatch—her seal plate blackened, its edges buckled by the blast.

Sera touched the ruined metal, and it sang back a low, embarrassed note. She laid both palms on it and breathed once, twice.

The glass beneath her skin answered, ember-lines brightening.

She pushed and the warped plate softened.

She peeled it up like bread crust.

Inside, the vent gallery was a narrow run between heat exchangers, now haloed in acrid smoke. Three figures crouched at the far end with crude charges and the kind of courage that grows in darkness and refuses to look into open flame.

"Stop," Sera said, and her voice filled the chamber the way heat fills a kiln.

Sudden, complete.

Two bolted and the third rose, tossing a spent detonator aside, and faced her.

He wore a rag wrapped over his nose; his eyes were young and sharp and convinced. "Traitor," he said.

Sera stood still. "To whom?"

"To the dead," he said.

"To my mother, who slept cold this winter because you hid the heat. To the children who will never see spring because you want to fire arrows at the sky."

The words lodged as they should.

Sera did not dodge them. "What's your name?"

"Panev."

"Panev," she repeated, tasting the shape. "You're right about the cold. Wrong about the arrows. I am building a bridge."

"To leave us behind."

"To carry those who can carry us forward."

She took one step closer, then another. He flinched but did not run.

"Do you think I have not counted your mother in my numbers? Do you think I do not count you now, standing here with ash on your tongue and fury where your breakfast should be?"

His chin lifted. "I think you have made yourself a god."

"No." She shook her head, and the embers in her hair flickered.

"I have made myself a witness who refuses to faint. And I am tired of praying to stars that do not answer faster than I can move."

He stared at her hands.

Scarred, steady, a woman who had carried hot metal through a lifetime and refused to drop it. Then his shoulders slumped, sudden as a structure when a load-bearing beam is removed.

"I don't want to die in the dark," he said, and he was a boy.

"You won't," she said.

"Not while the forges hold. Help me keep them steady, and if you are chosen, help me light the way for the ones behind you."

He looked past her toward the open hatch.

Danea's voice, clear and authoritative, cut above the bustle.

"Water to the left line! No, the old knees first; the young heal faster. Pan salts—now!"

Panev swallowed. "If I come with you now, what happens to the others? My friends."

"You bring them to me," Sera said.

"Or you ask them to meet me in the east court at dusk. I will tell them the truth in a voice that doesn't need a bomb to be heard."

He nodded, small and fierce and the detonator in his hand clattered to the floor.

Behind Sera, a new figure filled the hatch.

Broad, ash-dusted eyes burning not with conviction but with betrayal.

"Mother," Jonar said.

Sera did not turn. "I am working."

"You always are," he said.

"Working the city. Working the Council. Working the numbers until they agree with what you wanted to do in the first place."

Panev stiffened.

Jonar's gaze flicked to the boy, then to the blackened plate at his mother's feet. "You're negotiating with saboteurs now?"

"I am cooling a fuse," Sera said, "so I can light a sun."

Jonar laughed, raw.

"You've made poetry your alibi."

"And you've made anger your refuge," Sera replied, turning at last to face him. "It keeps you warm, I know. But it burns only you."

His jaw worked.

"You put Eris on the list."

"I did."

"She abandoned us."

"She sought a wind we could not give her."

Sera kept her voice level.

"I will not punish talent because it embarrassed tradition."

"She embarrassed you," Jonar snapped, and there it was: the old wound, sore as the day it first bled.

His daughter had chosen sky over forge; his mother had admired her for it.

Sera wanted to gather him as she had when he was small—when he migrated through moods like weather and only closeness could hold him to the ground. She did not move. He was a man with a city on his shoulders and a hurt boy inside his shirt; nothing but time and work could make them agree.

"Walk with me," she said instead.

"There is more to do than argue."

"I'm convening the Engineers' Assembly," he said. "We will petition to seize the capacitors under emergency statutes."

"You can try," Sera said evenly.

"But I buried them beneath bedrock that remembers earthquakes better than councils. You'll need half the city's blast reserves to reach them, and then we will have neither heat nor launch."

He stared at her. "I don't know who you are anymore."

"I am the woman who taught you that glass breaks along the line you cut," she said. "Choose careful lines, Jonar."

He left, anger moving in his wake like a pack of stray dogs. Panev watched him go, mouth a hard line.

"East court at dusk," he said, and ran.

By late afternoon, the East Court was a human forge.

Hundreds packed the amphitheatre steps; children sat on the warm stone with feet swinging, elders leaned on walking sticks that had been ribs of ships in another life. The air smelled of metal and cook broth, glow salt, and hair, the ordinary musk of a species that still insisted on living.

Sera stood without dais or staff.

Danea hovered at the edge with a medic's kit; priests lined the upper rings, some turned toward her, some turned away.

"I promised truth," Sera began.

"It is not a warm thing. It won't tuck you in. It will, however, give you hands to build with and a spine to stand with while the wind tests your courage."

She spoke of rationing and repair rosters; of clinics and child-heat priority; of the Flame Trees, whose sap could be tapped for emergency calories if cut at the right hour.

She gave schedules, who would shift sleep to match the launch window practice, who would smelt, who would sing. She assigned apprentices to elders whose hands shook and elders to apprentices whose hands flew too fast.

She named the dead, recent and old, and asked the living to say their names back to her, loud, so the forges could learn them and keep them warm a little longer.

She did not say I'm sorry. That was a gift that belonged in kitchens, not courts.

When she finished, someone on the middle tier clapped.

The sound multiplied, metal-on-metal, palm-on-palm, until it felt like standing inside a bell. Sera took it not as praise but as permission.

A runner shouldered through the crowd, breathless.

"Message from Zephara," he gasped, shoving a sliver of storm glass into Sera's hand.

She pressed it to her ear.

Tavir's voice, tattered by wind, filled the bone. "Sera— martial law. The council has seized the yards. I can keep three Arks hidden in the shadow channels, but we'll need a rise, not a roll. Straight up, hard and fast, or they'll track us. Can your capacitors deliver a spike as tall as God?"

Sera smiled, brief and unbeautiful. "Tell your god to mind his eyebrows."

She tucked the message into her bracer and looked up into the sky.

Brass and bruised, streaked with the exhaust of a thousand working days.

"Six weeks," she said to the court.

"We will turn a temple into a hammer and the sky into an anvil. And when the Third Bright comes, we will strike."

The court exhaled as one.

Acceptance?

Perhaps.

More likely fatigue finding a shape to rest in.

Danea stepped forward with a second slate.

"Another list?"

"No," Sera said.

"A letter."

"To whom?"

"To Eris."

Danea smiled, sudden and bright in the old way. "Ah."

Sera took the stylus. For a moment she saw her granddaughter at ten cycles. Sooty cheeks, knees scabbed, hair like spun copper trying to lift in a wind that wasn't there.

She wrote:

Child of mine.

I have put your name where the wind will see it. Come home. Bring the storm in your pockets. Your uncle is angry, and your grandmother is busy, and your mother is tired, and the world is ending. If you arrive before sunset, I will let you shout at me first.

Sera

She passed the slate to Danea.

"Send it with a hawk."

"We don't keep hawks," Danea said.

"Then borrow one from the Aerethi. They owe me a bird."

They both laughed, and in that small, reckless joy the city felt momentarily young.

Night fell and in the tunnels beneath the southern ridge, Sera and a team of engineers opened the first capacitor vault. The doors recognised her hand and unsealed with a hiss like a sigh held too long. Rows of glass-metal cylinders glowed inside like steady, sleeping suns.

"Mother," Danea said quietly, wonder and terror in equal measure, "how long have you...?"

"Since Jonar was still losing his baby teeth," Sera said.

"Since before Eris traced storms on the windows and Karo learned to hold a hammer without dropping it on his foot."

She placed her palm on one cylinder.

It warmed under her touch, answering the body it had been hoarded for.

Above them, bells tolled once, then again, slowly, heavily.

Not alarm.

Not breach.

The long bell that marked a birth or a death.

Sera closed her eyes.

Either was the truth.

Her comm-bead clicked.

A voice she loved more for its arguing than its agreement spoke into her ear. It was raw, hoarse, humbled.

"Mother," Jonar said.

"I have the Assembly. We'll hold the western vents if you give us the schematic for the transfer spines. We can't keep bleeding on both sides."

Sera leaned her forehead against the cool glass.

"I'll send it in a minute."

A final pause.

"And I'll put Karo forward for the thousand. He won't forgive me if I don't."

Sera smiled into the quiet.

"You are a better father than you think."

"Tell me that when he's in the sky."

"I will," she said, "and then I will tell the ground."

The line clicked off.

Danea squeezed Sera's shoulder.

"He bent."

"I told you," Sera said.

"Iron first. Then human."

They began the transfer.

The slow, disciplined ritual of waking caps and feeding them into spine conduits that would carry their charge to the catapult housings. The work sang through wrenches and seals, bolts, and breath. It sounded like Thalanor had always sounded: people who turn heat into form.

At the edge of Sera's awareness, a new sound joined the harmony—faint at first, then so clear it made the hair on her arms rise.

Three bright, pause, two dim, long silence, five.

Only this time it came from the earth, not the mirrors. The bedrock itself had learned the cadence.

Sera laughed a low, fierce sound that tasted like iron and freedom.

She pressed both palms to the conduit casing and spoke to a planet that had carried her whole life without once asking for thanks.

"Listen, old friend, we are going to ask you to do a terrible, beautiful thing," she said.

The conduit thrummed beneath her hands, as if the world was not merely willing but eager.

Above, Ember City glowed like a field of stars.

Below, the Heart of Ember turned its ancient face toward the sky.

And in the distance, over Zephara, lightning stitched a ragged seam the shape of a door.

Six weeks, Sera thought.

We will turn ashes into Skyfire.

And on the Third Bright, we strike.

CHAPTER 9

The Whispering Sky

Dawn came slowly over Zephara, painting the sky not gold but the colour of pewter and bruised glass. The wind, usually a friend to the Aerethi, carried an unfamiliar note—thin, uneven, like breath stolen from a dying song. The floating city drifted lower, its magnetic tethers straining, its towers humming with a sound that meant fear more than motion.

From the command deck of the Sky Ark Veyra, Tavir Kelen stood looking down at the world he might never see again.

Below him, Aurethis sprawled like a broken mosaic.

Once-glorious mirror fields cracked in the half-light, rivers of molten glass crawling between them like veins of gold bleeding into dust.

Every few seconds, the sun pulsed weakly.

Three bright, pause, two dim, long silence, five, as if it too had learned Kaedon's rhythm and was whispering the countdown back to its children.

Beside Tavir, Ryn, his eldest son, checked readings on the power lattice. "Stabilisers are holding for now," he said. "But the wind stream's thinning faster than forecast."

"How long before we start to sink?" Tavir asked.

"Three days," Ryn replied. "Maybe less if the currents collapse completely."

Tavir gave a low whistle.

"That's generous. The sky's getting sentimental."

Ryn's jaw tightened.

"You shouldn't be here. The Federation's patrols are looking for you. The Council declared you a traitor last night."

Tavir chuckled, shaking his head. "I was a traitor the moment I looked up and said the stars were closer than they pretended to be."

"Father..."

"Don't," Tavir said, more softly now. "We've had enough of that word for one lifetime."

The bridge lights dimmed, then flared back to life as the auxiliary generators compensated. Across the deck, Aerethi crew members worked with quiet urgency—hands flying over control boards, voices kept low, almost reverent. They knew what the Veyra was: not a ship, but a prayer with engines.

In the upper spire, Tahlia Kelen, Tavir's middle daughter, watched the horizon through the storm glass observatory. Diplomat by title, dreamer by defect, she had always believed the wind could be negotiated with. Now she wasn't so sure.

Her mother, Nivara, joined her. "He's pushing himself too hard," she said.

Tahlia didn't turn. "You could say that about everyone who's still trying."

Nivara exhaled. "You sound like him."

"I learned from him," Tahlia said. "And from you."

They stood in silence for a moment, the faint vibration of the engines thrumming beneath their feet.

Outside, Zephara's smaller islands drifted nearby.

Tethered habitats, storage silos, the great refuelling platforms of the Sky Federation. Soldiers were already moving across the bridges connecting them.

Martial law had turned the air routes into veins of patrols.

"Once we launch," Nivara said, "there'll be no coming back. You understand that?"

"I do."

Tahlia's gaze never wavered. "But I also understand what happens if we don't."

By midday, Tavir gathered his core officers in the wind-chamber. The circular hall, where every sound became a harmonic, and the air itself could be made to sing.

The walls trembled faintly, tuned to the frequency of the ship's engines.

"Kaedon's confirmed the window," Tavir began.

"Six weeks. When the Third Bright flares, we rise. That's our only chance to escape the gravity well before the upper currents collapse completely."

A murmur ran through the room.

Someone whispered.

"Six weeks?"

Someone else muttered.

"We'll never finish the stabiliser lattices."

Tavir raised a hand. The air quieted. "I didn't ask for permission to succeed. I asked for courage."

That silenced them more effectively than a command.

"We'll need fuel plasma from the Thalanor and mirror calibration from the Solenari," he continued. "Lumera's sending converters through the mirror network—when they arrive, integrate them into our navigation array immediately. The Arks must align with Kaedon's coordinates the moment the window opens. If we miss even a fraction of the phase, we'll fly blind into the dark."

"Where are the other ships?" asked Captain Renn, his second. "The Zephyrion and Lanneth?"

"Hiding in the shadow currents south of Zephara," Tavir said. "Once we draw Federation eyes here, they'll climb free. They're counting on us to be the lightning rod."

Renn grimaced. "And what happens to us?"

Tavir smiled crookedly. "We catch fire."

The night crept in like a bruise spreading across the horizon and the city's glow dimmed to embers; even the sky seemed tired.

In his quarters, Tavir sat before the window, listening to the quiet thrum of the ship. His wife entered without knocking—an old habit from a life when privacy was something they could afford.

"You're thinking again," Nivara said.

"I never stopped."

"Then at least drink something while you do." She handed him a cup of heated mead, its scent sweet with spice and memory.

He took it, nodded his thanks. "Do you remember our first flight over the North Winds?"

She laughed softly.

"I remember thinking you were either the bravest man I'd ever met or the stupidest."

"And which was it?"

"Both." She leaned against the window beside him.

"I also remember thinking the world couldn't possibly end while the wind still sang."

Tavir looked at her, the years in her face illuminated by the glow of the dying light. "It still sings," he said. "Just softer."

Nivara reached out and brushed her fingers along his temple, tracing the faint streaks of silver.

"When we lift, I'll be in the co-pilot's seat. Don't you dare leave me behind."

He smiled. "Wouldn't dream of it."

The following morning brought chaos.

The Federation Patrol Corps breached the upper docks before dawn.

Sirens blared, echoing across Zephara's bridges.

Patrol skimmers darted between platforms, engines whining. Over the comms, Tavir heard the call: "By order of the Sky Federation Council, the Sky Ark Veyra is seized. Crew will stand down immediately."

Ryn swore under his breath.

"They found us."

"Then we make it hard for them to keep us," Tavir said, rising. "Tahlia—seal the west bridge. Nivara, fire the wind anchors. Renn, get the crew to lockdown positions. We're leaving now."

"You can't be serious. The Arks aren't flight-ready!" Ryn said.

"They're dream-ready. That's good enough." Tavir said.

The engines roared to life and energy surged through the conduits, storm glass veins lighting up like lightning caught in amber.

The Veyra groaned, its tethers straining.

Outside, Federation skimmers circled like hornets.

"You're disobeying a direct order..."

Tavir cut the transmission.

"I've always been terrible with directions."

The tethers snapped.

The Veyra lurched, dropping several hundred spans before the stabilisers caught. Every deck shuddered; warning lights flashed crimson. Then the ship rose again, shaking free of its moorings. The sky split open with wind and fury.

Through the viewport, Zephara receded. A shrinking crown of gold and glass.

Tavir felt the vibration change. The sound of defiance turning into ascent.

Nivara gripped the controls beside him. "You're enjoying this."

"Terrified," Tavir said, grinning.

"But yes."

Behind them, Ryn monitored the rising altitude.

"Crossing forty thousand spans. Magnetic turbulence increasing."

"Let her climb," Tavir said. "She was built for storms."

Outside, the wind screamed. Lightning licked the hull; the sky turned liquid and alive. The Veyra plunged through the cloud layers until the world below was only a dim smear of gold.

For a long moment, silence reigned.

Then, through the static, the ship's comm crackled.

"Tavir," a familiar voice said, low, steady, resonant. Kaedon.

"You've reached the first line. Hold there. The path begins where sound ends. Do you see it?"

Tavir scanned the instruments.

A faint shimmer appeared on the radar. A thin band of fluctuating light stretched across the void like a bridge woven of nothing.

"I see it," he whispered. "The Sky River."

"Then wait," Kaedon said. "Not yet. The window hasn't opened."

"Six weeks," Tavir murmured.

"Yes," Kaedon replied. "Six weeks to prepare. Six weeks to say goodbye."

The line went silent.

When the ship steadied, Ryn turned from the console. "What do we do now?"

Tavir looked through the viewport at the shimmer of that impossible path glinting just beyond reach.

He thought of Sera's forge, of Lumera's mirrors, of Kaedon's shadowed archive.

"We wait," he said. "And we build our courage to follow them."

He closed his eyes and listened.

To the hum of engines, to the whisper of air slipping over the hull, to the faint, impossible song of wind that came not from Aurethis but from something farther away.

It wasn't thunder.

It wasn't a storm.

It was the sound of another sky calling their names.

And Tavir Kelen, Chancellor of the Sky Federation, traitor of a dying world, smiled through his fear and whispered back.

"We're coming."

CHAPTER 10

The Council of Shadows

The caverns beneath Thrayne had always been places of silence. Now, they were filled with whispers that refused to die.

The Council of Shadows had convened an emergency session called without ceremony, without song. Its members gathered in the Black Hall, a chamber older than history itself, carved from solid obsidian whose surfaces absorbed more light than they reflected. The air shimmered faintly with heat and tension.

Kaedon Vareth stood on the centre dais, flanked by two guards who were there as much for appearance as containment. His cloak hung torn at the hem, the fine dust of the lower tunnels clinging to his boots. He had returned from the southern outfalls hours ago, tired, but alive, and carrying more truth than the Council wanted to hear.

Across from him sat the Twelve. Archivists, Dream-Scribes, and the Council's presiding head: Archivist Jorel, his old student turned reluctant adversary.

Jorel's expression was carved from composure, but his eyes betrayed the cost of it.

"Dream-Scribe Vareth," Jorel began, "you stand accused of disseminating false prophecy, endangering the stability of the Archive, and communicating with outside factions against Council directive. Do you contest these charges?"

Kaedon's voice was calm, almost gentle.

"I do not contest the words, only the meaning behind them."

Jorel frowned.

"Meaning?"

Kaedon took a step forward.

"I have not spread prophecy. I have spread evidence. I have not endangered the stability. I have reminded you that we are dying. And as for communicating with the outside, yes, I have spoken to Lumera, to Sera, to Tavir. Because silence will not save us."

A low murmur rippled through the chamber.

Some of the older Scribes nodded faintly; others turned away, as if his words might infect them.

Jorel raised a hand.

"You would make a rebellion sound like poetry."

Kaedon smiled. "Only because you mistake silence for peace."

From the observation gallery above, Evara and Lynis watched.

Below, Neriel stood ready beside the acoustic array—a set of glass conduits designed to carry the Council's decrees through the tunnels.

The array was supposed to amplify truth.

In practice, it made lies louder.

Evara's fingers tightened around the railing.

"He shouldn't have come back," she whispered.

Lynis tilted her head.

Her eyes were sightless, but she could see the tension in Evara's breath, the tremor in the metal beneath her hand.

"You know he would never leave without singing the last verse himself."

Evara's voice cracked.

"He's too old for martyrdom."

Lynis smiled faintly.

"No one is ever old enough to avoid it."

Below, Jorel was still speaking.

"The Council has reviewed your findings," he said, "and concluded they are... anomalous. Coincidences of resonance, not communication. We cannot sanction mass panic based on unproven phenomena."

Kaedon laughed softly.

The sound echoed strangely, as if the stone itself wanted to laugh with him.

"Unproven phenomena? Tell me, Jorel—when you were my apprentice, did you not once say that proof is the child of curiosity and courage? When did you become afraid of your own words?"

Jorel's face twitched, but his tone remained smooth.

"I became responsible for more than myself."

"Then act like it. You have heard the rhythm. You've seen the reflection. The world is ending, Jorel. Pretending not to hear the roar doesn't make the lion vanish." Kaedon said quietly.

Jorel's patience cracked.

"Enough. You will hand over all data related to the Mirror Code and your communication logs with foreign agents. The Council will oversee the information's preservation."

"Preservation? You mean burial." Kaedon repeated.

He reached into his cloak, and for a moment, the guards tensed.

But he withdrew only a small crystal, faintly glowing, one of Lumera's converters, encoded with the harmonic frequencies.

Its pulse illuminated his hand like captive starlight.

"This," Kaedon said, raising it for all to see, "is proof that we are not alone. Not in ignorance, not in despair, and not in the universe. Lumera forged it from light. Sera feeds it with flame. Tavir carries it in the wind. Together they form the key to Illumeris—the Second Sun."

Gasps rose from the gallery.

The younger scribes leaned forward, eyes wide, hungry for belief.

Jorel stood. "Seize him."

The guards hesitated.

"Do it!" Jorel snapped.

They stepped forward, but before they could move, the floor beneath them trembled.

The obsidian pillars thrummed with a low frequency that shook the chamber like a great throat clearing itself.

Dust fell from the arches.

Kaedon's eyes widened. "Do you feel that?"

One guard froze.

"What is that sound?"

Lynis answered from the gallery above, her voice clear and cutting through the noise:

"Three bright, pause, two dim, long silence, five."

The cadence rippled through the hall.

The pillars pulsed faintly in response.

The same rhythm Kaedon and Lumera had discovered.

Kaedon turned slowly toward Jorel.

"The planet is speaking, old friend. You can call it a coincidence if it helps you sleep."

The younger scribes broke ranks, whispering among themselves, some already running for the lower corridors. They wanted to see it, to hear it for themselves. The world's dying heartbeat sounded like a door knocking to be opened.

Jorel's voice rose over the chaos.

"Contain this madness!"

Kaedon stepped toward him, the crystal in his hand flaring brighter.

"Madness is thinking that we can hide from extinction and still call ourselves wise."

In the confusion, Evara moved.

She descended the spiral stair, cloak billowing like shadow against flame.

When she reached Kaedon, he turned to her, smiling that tired, unrepentant smile that had first made her fall in love with him half a century ago.

"You shouldn't be here," he murmured.

"I always am," she said, and took the crystal from his hand.

Guards closed in.

Lynis raised her staff, striking the floor once.

Sound exploded.

A resonance pulse that shattered two of the pillars' outer shells.

Obsidian fragments rained down, dazzling in their fall. The guards faltered, ears ringing.

Evara seized Kaedon's arm.

"The tunnels. Now."

He hesitated, glancing once at Jorel.

Their eyes met. One pleading, one full of regret.

"I'll buy you time," Jorel said quietly, barely moving his lips.

Kaedon nodded once.

"Then let's hope your misfiling skills are still sharp."

The tunnels of Thrayne were alive.

Every wall glowed faintly now, veins of blue-white light threading through the stone.

The Mirror Code had awakened something.

The resonance spread faster than Kaedon or even Lumera could have predicted. It was as if the planet itself had remembered a song it had been too afraid to sing.

Lynis led the way, tapping her staff in time with the rhythm.

Behind her, Darel carried the data slates and Evara the crystal.

Kaedon walked last, leaning heavier on his walking stick than he liked to admit.

At a junction, they paused.

Faint tremors shook the air.

"That's the Heart of Ember," Evara said.

"Sera must have begun the capacitor sequence."

"Good," Kaedon said, smiling faintly.

"Let the fire wake before the light fades."

From the far end of the tunnel, footsteps echoed—many, rapid, closing in.

Darel turned pale. "Council guards."

Kaedon glanced at Lynis.

"Can you collapse the side shaft?"

She nodded, striking the staff once more.

The ground moaned; the ceiling dropped in a cascade of stone and dust, sealing the path behind them.

Evara coughed through the smoke. "We can't keep running like this."

Kaedon looked down at Darel, whose hands shook as he clutched the slates. "Do you remember the cadence?"

Darel nodded. "Three bright, pause, two dim—"

"Good." Kaedon smiled.

"Keep it safe. If they take me, if they take any of us, you keep that rhythm. It's the pulse of what comes next."

They reached the outfall chamber. The same one Kaedon had used to send his last message. The great mirrored pool glowed with an inner light, as if the planet's veins had converged here to breathe. Above, a thin shaft opened toward the surface; faint daylight trembled through.

Kaedon turned to Evara.

"Go."

"Not without you."

"Always without me," he said gently.

"That's how we keep the story moving."

Lynis touched Evara's arm.

"He's right. Someone must take the crystal to the Crossroads. Lumera and Sera will be waiting."

Evara hesitated, torn between duty and a love that had outlived the comfort of years.

"And you?"

Kaedon smiled.

"I'll stay and argue with anyone who still thinks silence is safer than truth."

He kissed her forehead, warm, lingering, the kind of kiss that felt like punctuation, not farewell.

Then he turned toward the pool, lifted his staff, and began to sing and the walls trembled with his voice.

It was not beautiful—it was old, cracked, carrying the weight of every unspoken word in a dying language.

The water responded, rippling in perfect counterpoint.

The rhythm of the Mirror Code echoed: three bright, pause, two dim, long silence, five.

Evara and Lynis climbed into the lift shaft with Darel between them.

The last thing they saw as they ascended was Kaedon standing in the reflected light, his silhouette dissolving into a thousand fragments of gold and shadow.

The guards reached the chamber seconds later.

Jorel was with them.

He raised a hand.

"Hold."

The men stopped, startled by the sight before them.

The Dream Well had come alive.

From its depths rose a column of light that reached toward the heavens—a bridge between stone and sky.

Within it, Kaedon's form flickered like a candle in the wind.

Jorel stepped forward, his face illuminated by the glow.

"Kaedon," he whispered. "What have you done?"

Kaedon's fading voice carried through the light.

"I have reminded the world how to dream."

And then he was gone as he folded into the brightness, leaving only the sound of water and the faint echo of the cadence in the walls.

Aboveground, in the dim twilight of the dying sun, Evara emerged with Lynis and Darel. The air tasted of iron and distance.

In the far sky, a faint column of gold rose from the heart of Thrayne, piercing the clouds.

Lynis turned her face toward it, eyes unseeing yet full of awe.

"He opened the first path."

Evara clutched the crystal to her chest.

"Then we carry the rest."

Darel looked up at the sky, his voice trembling with something that might have been hope.

"Do you think he's gone?"

Evara smiled through tears that caught the last light.

"No, he's gone ahead."

The wind shifted—warm, rising from the south.

It carried with it the scent of metal, smoke, and new beginnings.

Far above, in the thinning sky, a shadow moved, vast and slow, the Sky Ark Veyra, banking toward the horizon, following the pulse of light Kaedon had left behind.

And in the depths of Aurethis, the planet's heart hummed in answer.

Three bright. Pause. Two dim. Long silence. Five.

The rhythm of survival.

The rhythm of hope.

CHAPTER 11

The Equinox Crossroads

There is a place on Aurethis where the world remembers how it was made. The Equinox Crossroads lies at the seam between plateaus and plains, where the twilight basins lift their dark mouths toward the wind islands that drift like patient whales.

Four elements meet there—sunlight, shadow, storm, and heat—and an old accord says that any who step within its boundary must lay down their flags and speak as kin.

The boundary is not a wall, but a geometry: a ring of fused glass that glows when the sun touches its edge, pocked with vents that breathe warm air from below and crowned with pylons that sing when the wind is right. In the centre stands a low dais of mirror-stone, black and bright at once, reflecting the sky even when the sky has nothing left to give.

Lumera Sael arrived first.

She came on foot from the last relay tower of Aurion's Edge, her robe darkened by travel, copper-thread mantle streaked with dust.

The morning light looked sickly and obliging, but the Crossroads made a feast of it, bending it through prisms whose names had been lost to history. She stepped into the ring and felt the old law settle around her shoulders like a cloak: you are here to remember the world, not to win it.

Taren had begged to come.

She had said no.

At the edge of the plateau, they had stood with foreheads touching as if the minor exchange of warmth could delay anything at all—death, duty, dawn.

"Bring me back a sky," he had whispered, half play, half prayer.

She had promised what no one had the right to promise and set out, anyway.

She lifted her hand, palm open.

The mirrors embedded in the ground answered with a faint harmonics check—her forge signature recognised, her presence recorded. Above her, the pylons wavered and settled, the strings of the world's instrument tightening to the key to work.

A figure moved at the Crossroads' southern edge, heat shivering the air around her long before her feet crossed the line.

Sera Thal came like a forge taking breath.

She wore travelling leathers, soot-dark with the ghost of a thousand small fires. The ember-threads beneath her skin pulsed with the steady assurance of a woman who had carried iron through a lifetime and learned which parts of herself would not bend. Danea walked beside her, carrying a tube of schematics; two Thalanor engineers followed, quiet as anvils.

"Light-sister," Sera said, clasping Lumera's forearms.

Her palms were hot.

"You look like someone who hasn't slept since the gods were young."

"I keep forgetting to schedule that," Lumera said, and they smiled the way old friends smile in a language that pulls pain out of the sentence and tucks it behind the punctuation.

Then the wind changed.

It arrived like laughter trying not to be heard.

Tavir Kelen skimmed in on a glider whose frame hummed with stolen lightning, banking at the last moment to alight on the ring with theatrical disrespect for gravity.

Nivara stepped down behind him without drama, the pilot to his storm. Ryn followed in a second craft and kept his distance because love sometimes needs room to breathe.

"Forgive the entrance," Tavir said, out of breath and pleased with himself.

"The Council suggested I remain indoors. I misheard."

"You always were bad at instructions," Sera said, eyes dancing.

"Only when they're wrong."

Tavir returned, and then, more quietly, to Lumera.

"Any word?"

She understood the question beneath the question.

"He sent the cadence. And then he went where we all intend to go."

Tavir's jaw worked.

He breathed once, sharply, as if the cabin pressure had just changed.

"Then the old man got there first."

"Someone had to open the door. He preferred polite knocking." Sera said.

They stood together on the mirror dais.

The Crossroads listened.

Shadows pooled at its northern edge.

In the soundless place where darkness kept its intelligence, a slight figure stepped forward, staff tapping a meter that did not belong to footsteps at all.

Lynis Vareth entered the ring like a note finally resolving.

Evara walked at her side; Darel followed with a pack too large for his frame and a new authority in his gaze. Lynis turned her face toward their friends, unseeing and unerring.

"Kaedon asked me to tell you he has stopped arguing and started travelling," she said. "He suggests you take this as both a warning and permission."

"Did he..." Tavir began and stopped because there was no good grammar for the absence Kaedon had chosen.

Evara reached into her cloak and drew out the crystal that had turned the Council into spectators, Lumera's converter, now wrapped in a Varethine binding cloth embroidered in ripples and spirals.

"He gave me this and a look that broke my heart and stitched it up in the same moment." she said.

Lumera took the bundle with both hands.

Her mirrored pupils threw back Evara's face and the faint blue of the converter's pulse. The crystal was warm, as if it had decided to believe in body temperature. She set it on the dais. The stone accepted the gift and sent a thin ribbon of light into the air.

"All right," Tavir said softly, the bravado drained into something cleaner.

"Let's make a new sky."

They worked as if the sun had agreed to wait.

It had not.

Lumera knelt at the dais, interfacing her converter with the Crossroads' old grid, fingers moving in the ritual of genius. Lines of light rose one by one, forming a fragile lattice that trembled in the untrustworthy morning.

Sera spread the schematics across the glass in a constellated map. Transfer spines, catapult housings, and rise injectors scrawled in the square hand of someone who writes to be built.

"Your capacitors will split their charge through nine conduits," Lumera said, tracing the paths.

"Three to each Ark's primary throat, two to auxiliary couplings, and here one to the mirror array. The array must be blinded for a breath while we open the window, or it will try to reflect the flux back into the ground."

"Back into the ground," Sera murmured, angry at physics for its lack of manners. "Understood."

Tavir stood back-to-back with Nivara and Ryn, installing Aerethi phase vanes into the lattice—thin petals of storm glass that would flex under high current and keep the rising ships from bucking themselves apart.

"These aren't pretty," he said, not as an apology but in honesty.

"They'll hold until the third bright. After that, we're in the mouth of whatever story Kaedon left us."

"Story," Lynis repeated, testing the word as if it were a lever. "Let me set the pitch."

She raised her staff and struck once, then again.

The pylons surrounding the ring answered with a harmonic that turned the air to living glass.

Three bright, pause, two dim, long silence, five.

The ring warmed beneath their feet; vents opened along its seam, breathing slow heat into the day. In the shadow of the northern boundary, the sound moved like water through rock.

"Will it hold?" Danea asked quietly. "The law of this place?"

"The Crossroads remembers older promises than armies," Evara said.

"But remembering and enforcing are cousins who don't always write."

As if to answer, dust lifted along the western road.

A column of riders approached, Solenari, by the look of their braided light-sashes, and behind them the rigid silhouettes of mirror guards.

On the eastern rise, Aerethi patrol skimmers hovered and declined to cross the ring.

From the south, grim and slow, came the Engineers' Assembly of Dravonar, with Jonar at their front in a cloak still stained with the memory of accusation.

"Stay within the circle," Sera said simply.

The first to dismount was Mother Veira of the Lumen Council.

She was young as councils go, old as light.

She stepped to the boundary and bowed just deep enough to be lawful.

"High Engineer Sael," she called, deliberately using a title the Council had stripped at dawn. "You stand under edict."

"I stand under the sky," Lumera replied without heat.

"If you break an accord older than your chairs, you will look smaller, not larger, by the time you are finished."

Veira's mouth tightened.

She looked past Lumera to the lattice.

"You intend to blind the mirrors."

"Only long enough to teach them a better trick," Lumera said.

"They'll thank me in the manner of instruments."

"By complaining forever," Tavir said brightly.

Veira's gaze flicked to him with that particular Solenari combination of condescension and admiration.

"Chancellor Kelen. Your thefts are well documented."

"Then you may keep the documentation," Tavir said. "I prefer ships."

On the southern side, Jonar halted just outside the ring, the law of the place stopping him where no guard could have. He met Sera's eyes and did not look away. The hurt still lived there; the pride did too.

"You'll receive the transfer spine schematic I promised," he called.

"The Assembly will reinforce your catapult housings if you accept Engineer oversight on discharge valves."

"Accepted," Sera replied at once, because victory that refuses compromise dies of vanity. "And I'll send you the updated rise-temperature tolerances. We lifted the ceiling. Light will need more heat than prayer."

A flicker crossed his face.

Respect, unwilling and clean.

"You always said so."

Between them, a courier staggered into the ring, legs shaking with the arrogance of distance. She carried a leather tube with Aerethi knots double-wound and sealed in red glass.

"For Sera Thal," she panted.

Sera took the tube and cracked the seal.

Inside, a narrow strip of storm glass trembled faintly with living charge.

A hawk's message.

She pressed it to her brow so it could taste her and then to her ear so it could sing.

A laugh leapt out of her, raw and delighted.

"The child is a storm with feet."

"Eris," Danea said, half a prayer, half a warning.

"She's coming," Sera said, showing the strip.

The glass carried the briefest scribble only Sera would call handwriting: On approach from western shadow lane. Three skimmers. Don't die before we argue. —E.

"Good. Arguments are a renewable resource." Tavir said.

On the north, a movement in the shadow line pulled Lynis' head to attention. Varethine figures slipped in along the cool edge of the ring, Shadow Walkers, faces unreadable, steps soundless.

At its centre, Archivist Jorel approached alone, hands visible.

"You misfiled well," Evara called, not kindly, not unkindly.

"I misfiled truth long enough to deliver it," he answered, stopping at the bright seam.

He bowed to Lynis. "Dream-Interpreter. You have my staff if you need its tip."

Lynis tilted her head. "We always do."

Veira, Jorel, Jonar, Tavir's skimmers—all of them, for a brittle moment, shared the same air without drawing blood.

The pylons sang a warning note whenever a foot drifted too near the ring's edge, and the ring held.

"Let's show them," Lumera said.

She placed Evara's converter at the centre of the dais and spoke the cadence. The lattice of light climbed higher, and with it a shadow-lattice rose as if reflected from beneath the earth. They crossed, refused each other, crossed again. The air took on the scent of rain where there was none. In the lattice's helix, points brightened and dimmed—the windows Kaedon had pulled from song—and finally, at a particular interval, the lattice bent toward a fixed place in the air and held, like a compass that has loved a north.

"There," Lumera said.

"That is where the rise must aim. Sera, your spike must last thirteen counts beyond what your engineers call sane. Tavir, you'll take yaw on count nine, pitch on count eleven. Nivara, you'll kill your corrective instincts at ten or the river will spit you out like a seed."

Nivara grinned, showing her pilot's teeth.

"I've always wanted permission to be wrong at the right time."

"And we?" Mother Veira asked, eyes on the helix, all argument temporarily burned to awe.

"What do the mirrors do when they are suddenly offered a sky they cannot hold?"

Lumera looked at her with the tenderness you reserve for old adversaries who taught you many necessary lessons.

"They do what they were always meant to do: they remember. Stand your choirs at the field edges. When the rise ignites, you will sing the mirrors into stillness. Tell them this light is not for keeping. Tell them it is for sending."

Veira closed her eyes as if the idea hurt.

"Sung stillness," she whispered. "Blasphemy with impeccable phrasing."

When she opened them, something almost like a smile touched her mouth. "Our voices will be ready."

"Engineers!" Jonar barked southward, decision made.

"Spine pattern seven. Double-sleeve the discharge valves. If anyone says 'safe,' report them to me for reassignment to kitchen fires."

Sera snorted. "He was born for this."

"He was born for you and learned the rest," Danea said.

A shadow swept across the ring.

Three Aerethi skimmers cut the western wind and dropped to the ground with more elegance than the Federation deserved to witness. Eris jumped from the first before it had fully settled, hair a wild weather report, boots dusty, eyes blazing in that particular Thalanor hue that looks like molten coin.

"Grandmother," she said, and Sera opened her arms and braced her ribs because love at that velocity is an impact sport.

Eris hit her, hugged her, then held her out at arm's length.

"If you put me on a list without asking, I reserve the right to survive out of spite."

"Approved," Sera said.

Eris turned, already searching the ring with the immediacy of a person built to coordinate motion.

"We'll need a wind song overlay on the rise to keep Zephara's patrols deaf at the moment of ignition," she said to Tavir without preamble. "We'll fly the Veyra as noise while the Zephyrion and Lanneth climb in shadow."

Ryn barked a laugh. "She's your kin, Chancellor."

"Not my side," Tavir said cheerfully. "The competent one."

Eris pivoted to Lumera, eyes on the lattice.

"I can read that well enough to be afraid. If your count slips by one, our stomachs will become anecdote."

"Then our count will not slip," Lumera said, and the steadiness of her voice made Eris nod because competence recognises its own religion.

Someone at the rim shouted.

Distant on the plateau, a line of Federation patrol skimmers stitched the horizon like a poorly conceived seam. On the southern plain, a column of Thalanor hardliners marched with banners that wanted to be weapons. In the east, a faction of Solenari zealots raised mirror-shields as if reflection could cut.

The pylons moaned, a low, warning chord.

"The ring holds," Lynis said. "The law still lives."

"Then let's not waste its breath," Sera murmured. "We have four thousand to choose and six weeks to teach them how not to die while we try not to die."

"Five weeks, six days," Evara corrected softly, glancing at the converter's slowing pulse. "Time's shoulders are narrow."

They began the litany.

They chose names.

Not the easiest, not the safest.

Names that fit together into a shape that could make a world: welders to kiss broken metal; midwives to teach breath; farmers who could persuade stubborn soil; poets to keep grief from drowning courage; pilots, navigators, healers, cooks; a child who had figured out how to grow mushrooms in the dark with only songs for light; an elder who knew one thousand ways to tell the truth so that it could be heard.

Mother Veira gave them a choir-captain whose voice could calm mirrors.

Jorel sent three scribes who were done with careful.

Jonar added Karo, jaw set like a doorframe.

Sera added two orphans who had learned to sleep beside heat wells.

Tavir promised half a dozen wind-techs who could fix a vane with their eyes closed and their hands tied.

Evara named a librarian who remembered the recipes that had kept the first winter from becoming a story we did not survive.

They wrote the list on three mediums at once because Kaedon had taught them to doubt single points of failure: crystal, stone, and mouth.

Lynis sang the names into Darel's ear until his breath learned them.

Darel recited until the pylons hummed along.

When the first thousand were chosen from each people, the lattice over the dais flared as if the world approved of arithmetic when it finally served something other than denial.

The twin-spiral sigil spilled onto the glass like a blessing burned into the floor of Lumera's tower long ago.

Sera closed her eyes and saw Kaedon in the light.

Tavir kept his open because some people are made to steer grief the way they steer wind.

Evara pressed her palm to the stone and felt a warmth that answered by knowing her name from when it had been small and new.

"Now we test the hammer," Sera said.

She raised her staff and looked to Jonar. "Spines?"

"Primed," he said.

"Conduits?"

"Hungry."

"Tavir?" Sera asked.

"Engines hot," he replied. "Arks listening."

"Lumera?"

She set the converter's face toward the south and lifted her hand.

"On my count," she said, and the world leaned closer.

Three bright.

The pylons shone.

The ring flushed to gold.

The vents exhaled heat that tasted like bread.

Pause.

The lattice trembled.

Sera felt the ache in her forearms that meant the catapult housings were asking to be loved gently and lied to.

Two dim.

Shadows crossed the helix.

Lynis' staff sang dissonance until the air agreed to behave.

Long silence.

The silence was not empty.

It was a road.

Five.

"Rise," Lumera whispered.

From the southern plain, a contained sun woke.

Heat surged through the conduits, roared up the spines, and clawed at the morning.

The ground shook, but the ring held.

The lattice bent toward its fixed point and, for a heartbeat that felt like the planet had forgotten how to breathe, the Crossroads became a column of light taller than God.

On the horizon, the Federation skimmers broke formation, confused by a sky that suddenly insisted on being louder than command.

The zealots lowered their mirrors because mirrors know when to surrender. The hardliners stopped marching and stared because even anger has a liturgy that must wait for wonder.

Tavir's wrist-comm flashed.

Nivara's voice filled his head.

"Spike looks clean. We can ride it."

"Don't," he said, grinning like a boy and a thief.

"Not yet. Make them watch us practice. Let the fear settle into their bones, where the rules live."

The column faded.

The ring cooled by centimetre.

The pylons let their notes fall, satisfied and a little smug.

Sera leaned her weight against her staff and laughed once, short and relieved. "Again," she said. "Tomorrow. And the next day. Every day until the Third Bright. We will teach the sky to expect us."

"Bring your choirs," Lumera called to Veira.

"Bring your scribes," Evara called to Jorel.

"Bring your rage where it can be turned into work," Sera called to Jonar.

"Bring your best arguments," Tavir called to everyone. "We'll need them for the parts of space that are boring."

They broke only when the light began to fail.

The Crossroads dimmed to its old twilight. The ring's glow sank into its seam. The pylons hummed a lullaby older than empires.

At the edge of the boundary, Veira paused.

"Kaedon Vareth," she said softly, eyes on the faded column's ghost. "Was he always like that?"

"Yes," Lynis said. "And more."

Jorel lingered long enough to commit a small heresy. He bowed toward the dais. "Forgive us our carefulness," he said to the air and the stone and the woman who had once taught him that definitions were obedient only to wonder.

When the four stepped out of the ring, the law let go of their shoulders.

The world resumed its bickering.

Lumera looked back once.

The mirror dais held the faintest reflection of a second sun, so dim you could call it imagination. She refused to. She touched the converter at her chest and felt its slow pulse answer—a heartbeat sent from shadow through light.

"Six weeks," Tavir said at her shoulder.

"Five weeks, six days," Evara corrected again, and Sera snorted.

"Plenty," Lumera said, and even she laughed at that.

They turned their faces to their corners of the dying world—plateau, cavern, forge, wind—and began the work that makes disbelief ashamed of itself.

Above them, the sky thinned.

Far out along the invisible river, something brightened as if at a remembered name.

And under the Crossroads, in a seam the planet had learned to hold open, the faint echo of an old man's voice went on teaching the silence how to sing.

CHAPTER 12

The Froge of Hope

The last flare before the Third Bright painted Aurethis in light that hurt to look at. Every mirror, every shard of obsidian, every drifting island caught the dying sun and threw it back, a slow uncoiling blaze that turned the planet into its own requiem.

At Aurion's Edge, Lumera Sael stood on the balcony of her tower, eyes veiled against the brilliance.

The mirrors she had once commanded now hummed with independence, angled to catch and hold the coordinates of the sky river. They did not obey her; they remembered her.

And that, she decided, was better.

Below, workers in copper-thread tunics moved like dust motes in the molten light—loading converter cores onto glide craft bound for the southern plains.

Each core thrummed faintly, like a caged heartbeat, waiting for release.

A small voice pulled her from thought.

"Grandmother?"

Elen stood beside her, barely tall enough to see past the railing.

The child's braid glinted white gold in the sun.

"You promised I could see the Arks when they rise."

"You will," Lumera said. "You'll see them blaze across the sky and vanish into forever."

"Will you go with them?" the girl asked.

Lumera smiled—a small, aching thing.

"My hands belong here, love. Someone has to make sure the light leaves properly."

Elen considered this in the solemn way children weigh truth. "Then I'll wave so high they can see me."

Lumera bent and kissed her hair. "Then they'll know where to find home."

Far below, in Dravonar's ember plains, the forges beat like drums.

Sera Thal moved among her engineers, her heat mantle flaring with each command. The Heart of Ember was awake now—its massive conduits glowing from within, heat shimmering off molten rivers that once slept quietly beneath the crust.

"Channel four sealed," Jonar reported, voice strained through the comm-static. "Pressure climbing to eighty percent."

"Hold at ninety," Sera replied. "If it exceeds a hundred before the Third Bright, we'll lose the containment web."

"And if we don't push it, the Arks will never reach escape velocity," Jonar countered.

Sera's eyes met his across the forge floor with pride and stubbornness reflected in each other.

"Then we balance on the line," she said. "The world has been doing it since it was born."

He almost smiled. "You always did like living dangerously."

"Danger is just the cost of living long enough to matter," she said. "Now keep the fire breathing steady."

As she turned back to the main array, Danea approached, a slate clutched to her chest.

"Mother. Word from the Crossroads. The Solenari choir has begun their songs of stillness. The mirrors are responding."

Sera nodded. "Then the sky will listen."

Danea hesitated. "And Kaedon?"

Sera's voice softened. "He's the silence between our words. That's where all stories live."

In the high sky, the Sky Ark Veyra drifted on borrowed patience.

Tavir Kelen leaned over the navigation table, eyes scanning the holographic map projected by Lumera's converters. The path to Illumeris pulsed faintly, a spiral corridor through folding light, anchored by the cadence Kaedon had left them.

"Ryn," Tavir said, "trim yaw by point three. Nivara, keep us on the lower current. The moment the Third Bright flares, we ride the river."

Ryn's voice was tight.

"We still haven't confirmed stable harmonics across the hull. The storm glass is singing at double pitch."

"Then it's happy. Ships that don't sing are dead." Tavir said.

Tahlia approached, her face lit by the hologram's glow.

"The Federation's still watching from the cloud barrier. They've grounded their patrols but haven't moved. It's like they're waiting to see if we actually dare."

"Good, maybe they'll learn something useful about courage." Tavir said.

Nivara turned to him.

"Do you ever stop pretending you're not afraid?"

He grinned.

"If I did, I'd have to start thinking."

The wind outside shifted, a deep, resonant hum that made the hull shiver. The instruments flared gold.

"The Third Bright," Nivara whispered. "It's starting."

In the Varethine Archives, silence reigned.

Lynis stood alone before the Dream Well. Its waters no longer slept—they shimmered with images that rose and fell like the memories of gods.

She could hear Kaedon's voice in the stone's vibration, a melody that no longer required lungs.

"All suns die," the echo whispered, "but not all hearts forget how to shine."

Evara entered quietly, leaning on a walking staff.

"The outfalls are flooding with light. The tunnels won't hold much longer."

Lynis smiled.

"Then it is time."

She dipped her staff into the well.

The water climbed up its length, forming a spiral of silver and blue.

"Carry this to the Crossroads," she said. "When the world opens, pour it into the air. It will remember his name."

Evara hesitated. "And you?"

"I will stay," Lynis said. "Someone must close the book."

Evara's eyes filled, but she nodded.

"He'd be proud."

"No," Lynis said softly. "He'd argue."

She turned her blind face upward, listening.

The ceiling above the Archive cracked, releasing a shaft of golden light that split the dark like a revelation.

"The window is opening," she whispered. "Go."

The Equinox Crossroads burned like a star.

The pylons sang in unison, their notes forming an invisible bridge between the ground and the sky. Around the ring, hundreds stood—the chosen four hundred, the children of every nation, faces glowing with the reflection of a sun they might never see again.

Lumera's lattice arched overhead, refracting the flare into a column of liquid gold. The Veyra hovered at its edge, engines screaming against gravity.

Behind it, two smaller Arks, Zephyrion, and Lanneth, drifted into formation.

Sera's voice came through the comm.

"Capacitors full. Heart of Ember at maximum charge."

Tavir replied, "Then let's make a mess worth remembering."

From the edge of the ring, Darel raised the harmonic amplifier and began to sing Kaedon's cadence.

His voice trembled at first, but others joined, Varethine tones low and resonant, Solenari choirs harmonizing above them, Aerethi wind-harps weaving through it all.

The sound rose, layer by layer, until the Crossroads itself vibrated.

"Three bright," Lumera whispered.

The light column surged upward.

"Pause."

Every engine, every breath, held still.

"Two dim."

The Arks' thrusters ignited, storm fire twisting into controlled fury.

"Long silence."

The world waited.

"Five."

Sera shouted, "Ignite!"

The Heart of Ember roared, its energy shooting through the conduits in a ribbon of molten light.

It struck the Crossroads ring, feeding into the mirror lattice.

The ground shuddered and then released.

The Veyra rose.

Lightning cascaded around it, gold and white, curling upward into the newborn river of light.

Behind it, the Zephyrion followed, wings wide, singing like thunder.

The Lanneth climbed last, smaller but no less defiant.

The crowd cried out, not in fear, but in awe.

Children raised their hands as if to catch the sparks falling like stars.

Sera's eyes filled with fire and tears.

"Go," she whispered. "Tell them we were here."

Lumera shielded her eyes, watching as the ships climbed past the clouds, past the mirror haze, into the thin blue above. For an instant, they seemed to stop—caught between the pull of the dying world and the call of another.

Then the light bent.

The sky rippled, a curtain folding back, and the Arks vanished into the helix Kaedon had sung into being.

Only their contrails remained—three luminous scars across the heavens.

The Crossroads dimmed.

The pylons' song faded to a hum.

And silence descended—a silence full of meaning.

Later, as the horizon bled to ash, Lumera knelt by the mirror dais as her fingers traced the cooling glass.

"They made it," she said quietly.

Beside her, Sera nodded.

"Or they're still making it. Either way, they're moving."

Evara approached, her cloak stained with dust and light. "Lynis is gone. She closed the Archives."

"Then Kaedon won't be lonely," Lumera murmured.

Above them, the remnants of the Third Bright scattered like petals in a dying wind.

Somewhere beyond sight, three ships rode the invisible current toward a new sun—a second light waiting in the silence between galaxies.

And Aurethis, their golden world, exhaled one last time.
Its skies shimmered like molten glass.
Its seas turned to mirrors.
And in their reflections, for one heartbeat longer, the faces of all who had dared glowed like stars.

CHAPTER 13

Illumeris Rising

The river of light did not feel like motion. It felt like being remembered. The Veyra hung inside the helix as if suspended in a throat of glass, every gauge pinned to impossible and then settling again, like a heartbeat learning a new rhythm. Stars did not streak. They rearranged—subtle, patient, the way furniture moves between childhood and age so that you only notice when your shins bruise against memory.

"Hold on the count," Nivara said, hands light on the controls, voice steady enough to fool the ship. "Do not correct. Do not admire. Do not pray louder than the engines."

On her left, Tavir let himself breathe. The storm glass veins in the bulkheads hummed the cadence Kaedon had left them.

Three bright, pause, two dim, long silence, five.

Only now it folded inward, as if the road had become a room.

"Phase vanes holding," Ryn reported from the systems cradle. "Hull temperature nominal. If physics had feelings, it would be offended."

"Physics has feelings," Tavir said. "They're just slow to admit it."

The Zephyrion and Lanneth drifted aft and starboard in the river, not flying so much as being carried with exquisite consent. Each ship sang a slightly different harmony, and together they made something that might not have been music but could not be called noise.

Through the forward viewport lay no stars, no void—only the faint suggestion of direction. Then, without warning, the river inhaled.

"Here," Nivara whispered.

The helix pinched. The ships shuddered as if startled, instruments flaring red then green then a colour the Arks' designer had never imagined.

The view ahead unravelled into gold.

A sun, young, and firm, its light the colour of clean honey.

Beyond it, a blue-green pearl turned upon itself, veiled in cloud bands that did not yet know the taste of soot.

The Veyra quivered like a creature that had been promised a myth and found it waiting politely on the porch.

Ryn laughed, the sound you make when your chest cannot hold only air. "We're through. We're through!"

"Steady. Map the gravity well. Taste the winds at range," Nivara said, though her mouth had softened into something that would have been a smile given another centimetre of courage.

Tavir leaned closer to the glass. The planet's dayside shone with oceans the colour of old songs. Along one limb, a necklace of islands glimmered; on the dark side, lightning embroidered a continent with silver stitches.

"Kaedon," he said, not into any comm but to the habit of speaking to the dead as if they were simply elsewhere, "you polite thief."

A soft tone chimed.

The converter at the navigation altar warmed to a pulse not unlike Aurethis' old light, yet younger, quicker. Lumera's device had learned a new sun in one breath.

"It answers," Tahlia said from the sensor pit, wonder swimming up through her training. "Spectral class G—slightly hotter than home. Atmosphere reads... nitrogen-oxygen dominant, trace argon, water vapor heavy. Methane negligible. Ozone present."

"Life?" Tavir asked, the word careful as a cup.

"Biosignatures probable," she said. "Photosynthetic response on the daylight curve. Oxygen variance on the night-side storm cells."

"Probable is good enough to risk a future on," Tavir murmured. "Nivara—hold high orbit. Ryn—link with Zephyrion and Lanneth: we'll split a scout net. Tahlia, give me three landing windows with fuel-to-hope ratios that won't embarrass us."

A fresh voice cut across the deck channel.

Bright, impatient, wind dented.

Eris Thal.

"Or we do it the Aerethi way," she said from the Veyra's dorsal skiff bay, "and go see for ourselves."

Tavir did not turn. "Eris, dearest storm, if you launch without a read on thermal shear, your grandmother will personally ignite a new star to fetch you."

"Affirmative," Sera's voice arrived from memory, not radio, and the bridge laughed because even in another sky the matriarch found a way to be present. The laugh shook the fear out of their ankles and left only readiness.

"Skiffs stay docked. We fly as a brood until we know where the hawks are," Nivara said, gentler than the command required.

The planet turned.

The ships coasted along the sunlight like hands sliding down a warm banister.

On the Zephyrion, Captain Renn reported a ring of mountains bright as teeth along a western ocean.

On the Lanneth, Navigator Shai found a chain of island arcs that sang to the radar as if each wanted to be met first.

Data crowded the Veyra's table until the table had to give it order.

"We need an anchor," Tahlia said. "Somewhere to kiss the atmosphere, not bite it."

"Look for a gulf," Nivara replied. "Where land breaks its own fall."

Ryn tuned the visual.

The planet's terminator, the night yielding to day, revealed a crescent bay scalloped by reefs.

Inland, a green plain rippled toward low hills scattered with darker, stiff shapes that could have been forest or something like it.

"There," Tavir said. "That's a place that knows how to receive."

"Wind profile?" Nivara asked.

"Upper atmosphere thin but friendly—no razor shear. Mid-layers heavy with water. Ground winds moderate, veering east."

"Temperature?" Tahlia chimed.

"Twenty-two," Ryn said reverently; a number from an old poem.

Tavir took his first truly deep breath since the helix.

"We'll test the air with teeth before we swallow it. Drop an aerostat. Pollen, spores, corrosives. If it hisses, back away."

The Veyra released a seed of glass.

It fell like a promise and opened like a flower: petals of sensor film, a throat of siphon, a tongue of chemical hunger.

Data poured up the tether line: no immediate toxins; complex organic volatiles; salt spray spiked with iodine; aerosols that read like breath, not plague.

"It smells like oceans and honesty," Tahlia said, and then, embarrassed by her own poetry, added, "Parameters within safe exploratory range."

"Good," Nivara said, voice quiet. "Then we take a hand off the banister and test the stair."

She eased the Veyra into the upper air.

Atmosphere folded around the hull with the intimacy of cloth. Heat blushed the plates and faded. The ship shivered, then steadied. Clouds abraded the windows with soft hands. Below, the bay widened like an eye opening in a kind face.

"Deploy glider wing," Tavir said. "Let's feel what it means to belong."

The storm glass feather array bloomed from the Veyra's flanks and caught the air the way a smile catches an apology and turns it into laughter. The ship sang lower now, a contented purr.

"Skiffs. Pairs only. You don't go out of sight. You don't get clever. Bring back air, water, soil, a rumour of leaf. Go." Nivara said finally.

Eris was already in the cradle with Karo Thal, Jonar's son, strapping in with the hurry of the well-trained. "Ready," she said, words clipped not by fear but by delight's discipline. "We'll take the southern reef."

"Confirmed," Nivara replied. "Renn—north shoals. Shai—river mouth. Veyra stays high, mothering like an accusation."

Eris's skiff slid into air with a feline satisfaction. The bay smelled of salt, hot metal from the ship's skin, and something green that had never tasted forge or mirror. Karo whooped and then cut the sound into a competent report.

"Reef structures appear calcium-silicate," he said, professional enough to make Sera proud if the stars carried pride.

"Biota visible. Shapes consistent with filtering organisms. No predatory response to shadow. Water clarity six spans."

Eris lifted them along the reef edge. Sunlight broke into coins. Schools of bright, tight creatures turned as if deciding together had always been fashionable.

"I'm bringing the sea to my grandmother," she said, and Karo grinned. "And we'll take the sky to my father."

They skimmed lower. On a rock just above the wash, something with jointed stalks and soft crowns swayed, tasting the light. Eris touched down beyond the spray line and stepped out, boots sinking a centimetre into unfamiliar sand.

The air was... kind.

She stood still, then knelt and pressed her palm to the ground. It was cool in the shadow, warm where the sun had held a hand. When she stood again, her face was wet with something that wasn't spray.

A soft chime in her ear: Tahlia. "Skiff Two, we're seeing movement inland—wind in the grass or something that wants us to think it is. Don't play hero."

"Copy," Eris said, and lifted, banking toward the river mouth where the bay narrowed into a tongue of green.

On the Veyra, Tavir watched the little craft like a father refusing to place name and fear on the same shelf. Nearby, Tahlia's fingers danced through volumes of air and numbers, building a vocabulary of a world from its weather.

"Illumeris," she tried the word on her tongue, the name they had inherited by myth. "It's quieter than I expected."

"It's listening," Nivara said. "New places do."

"Can places hear?" Ryn asked, half-mocking, half-alone-with-his-thoughts.

"They can remember," Tavir said. "That's halfway to hearing."

The Zephyrion's comm lit.

"Captain Renn to Veyra. We have fresh water—sweet, mineral-light. We have clay—plastic, iron-poor. We have a stand of—trees?—if that's the word. Tall, jointed. Trunks, like braided reeds, hardened into wood. Leaves… no leaves, more like lattice fronds."

"Record, sample, bless," Tavir said. "Leave the grove as you wish to return to it."

From the Lanneth: "Navigator Shai reporting. Inland hills hold a darker band—basaltic, likely old volcanics. Magnetic flux minimal. No ferromagnetic surprises. We found prints by the river. Not claws. Pads. Four and a half spans between steps."

The bridge stilled.

"Large herbivore?" Tahlia ventured.

"Or a very polite predator," Ryn said.

"Either way," Nivara murmured, "we are not alone in the simple sense."

Eris's voice cut in, breathless but steady. "Confirm prints at South Delta as well. Similar size, shallower depth. Moving in a line that suggests migration, not hunt."

"Good," Tavir said. "Then let us be prey that behaves like a guest."

A chime from the converter altar—soft, persistent.

Tahlia glanced down.

The device had pulsed not with the cadence of Kaedon's map but with a slower, broader rhythm—an environmental match.

"It wants to speak to the sun," she said, astonished. "It's syncing to local flare harmonics."

"Can we piggyback?" Tavir asked.

"A beacon. Not back to Aurethis—the river doesn't run both ways—but to each other, if the Zephyrion or Lanneth drift beyond range."

"Shortwave reflection on upper ion," Ryn said, already tuning.

"We can lay a breadcrumb string along the thermals."

"Do it."

The Veyra breathed.

The ship had always been a machine; today it felt like a person refusing to apologize for the way it loved air.

"Captain," Nivara said softly, nodding forward.

On the horizon, the terminator line rolled over the bay.

Night on Illumeris did not fall; it arrived, a blue velvet spreading, pricked with unfamiliar constellations. The young sun slipped away, and in its place the sky deepened to a colour Tavir had not learned a word for.

The first star in that field looked, for a breath, familiar.

"Don't," Tahlia said quickly, already expecting the ache.

"It isn't ours. It only wants you to think so."

Tavir let the ache pass through. He had learned as a child that you cannot out-climb longing; you fold it, pack it well, and bring it with you so it won't trip you later.

"Recall skiffs," he said. "We camp in the high air tonight and choose our first ground at dawn. I want the Zephyrion over the river plain; the Lanneth over the reef. We triangulate storm behaviour and listen for things with teeth that don't sing."

As the skiffs returned, a tiny figure stood at the edge of the Veyra's hangar door, fists jammed into too-large pockets, eyes wide.

A child—one of the chosen thousand hundred: Lira Sael, Lumera's granddaughter, who had talked her way aboard with a pencil stub and a promise to "draw the wind."

Tahlia crouched. "You're supposed to be buckled in the family bay, artist."

"I was," Lira said, honest as rain. "But the sky is having a conversation, and I didn't want to be rude."

Tahir grinned despite himself. "What's it saying?"

"That we should be careful where we step."

Lira pointed toward the river plain. "Because there are stories there, and stories don't like to be stepped on before they finish themselves."

"Very well. We will ask permission in the morning." Tavir said solemnly.

Night opened its hands.

On the surface, heat rose off stone and water in secret.

The Veyra banked into a slow circle, a lantern hung from a new heaven.

Dawn on Illumeris was a colour the language of Aurethis had no drawer for.

It found the Veyra's hull and turned it to a quiet coin. The ships dropped a little, slow spirals to taste the day under less distance.

"First ground," Nivara said.

Tahir nodded. "Find us a cliff. Something that lets us look and be seen without looking like a promise we can't keep."

They found it at the mouth of the river, where the plain lifted its chin into a low bluff. Grass like sleek wire ran in wind-combed waves.

Below, the beach curved into the bay; above, the darker shapes that might be trees leaned slightly together as if telling gossip.

"Touch earth," Nivara said, and the Veyra settled with the care of a mother laying down beside a sleeping child.

The boarding ramp unfolded.

Air ran up it like greeting dogs.

Tahir stood at the threshold, hand on the jamb, and thought of every door he had ever opened: homes, council chambers, cockpits, the mouth of a storm. He thought of Kaedon stepping into a pillar of light as if it were a hallway he had simply forgotten to use for a while.

He thought of Sera's laugh when she promised to hammer the sky flat enough to walk on. He thought of Lumera's hands shaping brilliance until it behaved. He thought of Lynis listening to silence and teaching it to be a choir.

He looked back at Nivara.

She nodded.

He looked at Ryn.

He nodded too, unwilling tenderness making his mouth sour and his eyes bright. He glanced at Tahlia. She had already unsnapped her harness and tucked a coil of hair behind her ear like someone preparing to broker a treaty with a god.

"Eris, Karo," Nivara said on the ground team channel. "With me. Tahlia, bring two medics, a soil tech, and a poet."

"A poet?" Ryn asked, eyebrows up.

"Yes," Nivara said. "In case the land requires praise instead of apology."

They stepped down.

Boot.

Boot.

Boot.

Illumeris took their weight and did not complain.

The grass brushed their knees with a sound like pages turning. The wind smelled of salt and green and something faintly metallic, like clean blood or fresh tools. A small creature the size of a fist darted from one tuft to another, unimpressed by history.

Eris knelt, pressed her palm to the ground as she had on the reef, and murmured the simplest prayer Sera had taught every Thalanor child, no doctrine, just gratitude. Karo unpacked a soil kit and teased meaning from grains with tweezers and a grin.

Tahlia picked up a handful of sand and let it fall through her fingers. "Hear that?" she asked.

"What?" Ryn said.

"The silence," she replied. "It's not empty. It's attentive."

The poet, Mira Kelen, Tavir's youngest, opened a small leather book, put pencil to paper, and wrote without looking at either: We arrive like the idea of rain / and the earth considers us kindly / for a moment that might be called morning.

The wind shifted.

Out on the plain, something stood.

They saw it first as a hesitation in the grass, a ripple forgone. Then a back lifted above the waves: tall, dun-coloured, jointed limbs long as ship spars and tipped in hooves that spread like the bases of small trees. Its head, oh, its head, was narrow, elegant, eyes set far apart, ears swivelling cup-like toward the newcomers. From the crest of its spine, lattice fronds rose and lowered slowly, catching light and throwing it, mirrors that had learned humility.

It inhaled.

Nivara lifted her hand, palm out, fingers loose. "Stay small," she said softly.

The creature swayed once, a movement too graceful to be caution yet too careful to be indifference. It lowered its neck, sniffed the air the newcomers had already walked through, and exhaled a sound that belonged equally to flute and bellows.

"Greetings," Tahlia said, as if etiquette applied to miracles.

The animal turned one eye—enormous, dark, fathomless—upon them.

On its surface, they saw the Veyra, small as a toy, three people with hands open, a poet holding her breath. Then it moved, placing a hoof where their prints had been, and every hair on Tavir's arms stood up because that was not mimicry, not quite—it was recognition.

The prints were now not theirs alone.

A second shape rose farther out, smaller, perhaps juvenile, lattice fronds still unfurling like questions.

The larger lifted its head and made a soft clucking noise. The smaller approached, bold with safety.

"Back slowly. Let them own the moment." Nivara whispered.

They did and the two crossed the line where ship-shadow met full sun, stood, considered, then turned together and moved away with the unhurried certainty of beings who have never been hunted. Their tracks stitched the plain: a new grammar laid over old.

Eris exhaled. "Tell my grandmother they have no claws."

"Tell mine they have manners," Tahlia said, half-laughing and not unweeping.

Ryn leaned forward.

"Tell everyone: we are not alone, but we are not unwelcome."

Tavir closed his eyes and saw the Crossroads—Sera's staff, Lumera's lattice, Evara's crystal, Lynis' listening, Kaedon's light.

He saw Aurethis as it had been, a golden world, then as it would be now, dimming toward its last long breath. He chose a words-bare thought and sent it down the thin, tentative ion thread the converter could convince into being—not across interstellar distance to a dying sun, but across this new sky to the other Arks and to anyone already looking up:

WE LANDED.
AIR KIND.
WATER SWEET.
LARGE GENTLE THINGS.
BRING STORIES CAREFULLY.

The converter pulsed once. Far to the north, the Zephyrion pulsed back. Over the reef, the Lanneth laughed in code.

"Home?" Ryn asked, timid as a question and brave as a decision.

"Not yet," Nivara said. "First, we build kitchen fires. Then we will see if the word wants us."

Tahir took the poet's pencil and scratched a tiny diagram in the corner of Mira's page—the bluff, the river, a square for the first shelter.

His hand shook.

He let it.

"Name?" Tahlia asked.

Mira answered without looking up. "Crosswind."

"Too Aerethi," Ryn objected, smiling.

"Ember Bay," Karo offered, loyal.

"Mirror Plain," Lira said, thinking of a grandmother working at a forge of light in a sky she would not cross.

Eris tilted her head, listening to the wind like a person who had grown up arguing with it.

"Promise Bend," she said finally.

"Because we turned, and it held."

Nivara nodded. "Promise Bend."

They set the first stakes.

Not many.

Not deep.

The kind of stakes that ask the ground, not tell it.

As they worked, the sun climbed, and the ocean threw chips of light at them like congratulations.

Above, three ships hung in a clean sky. Below, feet pressed new grammar into a willing earth. Far away, across a dark now too long to speak across, a golden world finished a song.

Inside the Veyra, the wind-chamber found a new note. It did not belong to Aurethis. It did not belong to Illumeris. It belonged to journey—for the time between worlds is a country of its own, and the people who live there learn to carry both grief and awe without spilling either.

At dusk, Tavir climbed the bluff alone.

He stood where grass met rock and tried to imagine the map this hill would someday draw in a child's mind: here is where the first ship slept, here is where the gentle giant stood, here is where the poet said a word that fit.

He lifted his face toward the first star.

Not his.

Not theirs yet.

Only bright.

"Kaedon," he said into the very wide air, "we'll speak politely."

The wind answered in a language he had always understood.

Behind him, voices rose until the four thousand sounded like a village. Pots knocked.

Tools argued softly.

Someone sang off-key and did not apologise.

Children asked where tomorrow lived and pointed in all directions when told there.

"Welcome," Tavir said to the hill, the bay, the sky, the pair of animals watching now from the shadow of the reeds. "We will try to be worthy of your patience."

Night arrived, not as an absence, but as another kind of presence. On a table made of two crates and a stubborn board,

Mira set a lamp and read back the first entry in a ledger that historians would someday argue over and be laughed over by grandchildren.

Promise Bend, First Night.

We placed our hands on new ground, and it did not flinch.

We saw tall, gentle things that stepped in our prints until they became theirs.

The air reminded us not to boast.

We ate simple food, and it improved in the telling.

We spoke our old names, and the place did not object.

Tomorrow we will ask for more.

Tonight, we will sleep.

The ship's hum like bees that have finally found flowers.

She closed the book and kissed its spine because some rituals have to be invented quickly or they will not exist at all.

In the hangar, Lira drew the wind.

It looked like a creature with ribs made of laughter.

On the reef, light crawled up the lattice fronds of plants that had not yet agreed to be called trees.

On the plain, two large soft-hooved beings lay down with their heads in the wind and dreamed slowly, as if remembering had tides.

And in the curved, widening space between one sun and the next, an old promise kept walking, even after the feet that made it had learned to move in light.

CHAPTER 14

The Children of Promise Bend

The first morning on Illumeris came softly. The light arrived not with command but with curiosity. It seeped through the mist rising from the river, spilling gently over the grass like an artist testing the first stroke of a brush. The world seemed to breathe before it spoke.

Eris Thal woke first.

She had slept on the bluff's edge, one arm flung over her satchel of tools, her head resting against a crate labelled Mirror Components: Handle with Reverence. The label had faded in salt and sunlight, but she liked the words. Reverence had always been her grandmother's language.

She blinked, squinting at the horizon.

The bay caught the dawn and turned it molten. The reef creatures below shimmered in schools, and for a moment she thought she saw Aurethis again, that same colour of dying gold, until the breeze reminded her this world was alive.

"Still here," she murmured, as if the planet might have moved overnight.

Karo stirred beside her, hair a mess of red-gold curls, face marked with the smudge of a dream.

"Are we dead?" he mumbled.

"No, we're inconveniently alive," she said, grinning.

He laughed, and that laugh, uncoiled, unguarded, was the sound of survival turning into living.

By the time the sun climbed above the hill, Promise Bend was awake.

Smoke rose from makeshift cook fires. The smell of baked root bread and spiced grain drifted over the bluff. Someone had discovered that the local tubers could be roasted if soaked in seawater first; someone else had already named them star roots. The name stuck before breakfast was done.

Eris walked through the camp, counting faces.

Two thousand of the four thousand were here; the others remained aboard the Veyra, Zephyrion, and Lanneth, ferrying supplies and repairing stress fractures from the passage.

Every face she passed carried something of their home world. Solenari grace, Thalanor fire, Varethine poise, Aerethi mischief. Four people, one fire, burning under a new sky.

At the centre of camp, Tahlia Kelen coordinated the morning roll call.

Her data pad flickered with notes and coordinates, hair pulled into a top knot that refused the wind's arguments.

Eris approached. "Any word from your father?"

"He's still mapping the upper currents," Tahlia said.

"Ryn's monitoring orbital decay. The Veyra's holding steady, but they'll keep watch for another rotation before committing to atmospheric docking."

Eris nodded. "And Lumera?"

"She sent a transmission last night from what's left of Aurion's Edge. The mirrors are burning themselves into the ground. She said it's beautiful."

Tahlia's voice faltered. "She didn't say if she was safe."

Eris placed a hand on her shoulder. "Some people belong to the light. It's where they finish what they start."

Tahlia swallowed, then smiled. "Then she's home."

Later that day, Nivara Kelen descended from the Veyra with the First Council. The chosen elders were fewer now, but each carried the weight of many voices. Sera's daughter Danea for the Thalanor, Evara for the Varethine, Tavir, and Nivara for the Aerethi, and Eris herself for those who built from flame.

They met beneath a woven canopy of sailcloth, the air fragrant with river bloom and dust.

"We survived the crossing," Nivara began, her tone both weary and proud. "Now we must decide if we mean to merely live, or to begin again."

Evara unrolled a small chart, a rough topography sketched from orbital data. "The planet has seven major continents, two small polar caps, and weather cycles that suggest long seasons. The Crosswind Bay gives us warmth, fresh water, and the mouth of a river system that can carry us inland."

"Perfect for trade and disaster. We'll need barriers. Floods here could drown dreams." Eris said dryly.

Danea nodded. "We can build levees from fused glass. A gift of our ancestors' arrogance."

"Arrogance kept us alive," Evara said gently. "Let's not apologise for it yet."

Nivara placed her palm over the chart. "First priorities: shelter, food, communication. We'll seed the first orchard where the soil reads fertile. The Aerethi will manage weather kites for early warning. Thalanor engineers will handle energy conversion from solar and heat. The Varethine will map mineral veins and underground flow."

Eris leaned forward. "And culture?"

All eyes turned to her.

"Culture," she repeated. "We've brought survivors. But if we forget who we were. Our stories, our songs, the way Sera laughed or the way Kaedon wrote — then Illumeris wins by accident."

Evara smiled, weary but luminous. "Then you'll help me build the first Archive."

Eris nodded. "And the first stage."

By the third day, Promise Bend no longer looked like a camp — it looked like intent.

Windmills made from salvaged hull plates caught the breeze and sang soft chords. Solar arrays shimmered like sleeping dragons. Thalanor heat-pits smelted sand into glass bricks, and Varethine children etched their first mirrors, shaping them into small, deliberate circles that caught the young sun's smile.

At dusk, Tavir's voice came through the comm:

"To the settlers of Promise Bend — report your count, your health, and any reason you're not smiling."

Nivara answered:

"We're standing, eating, and occasionally laughing. That's all the report you'll get until you land."

"That's good enough," Tavir replied. "The Veyra will make descent tomorrow. I promised the ship I'd let her taste rain."

The transmission ended. For a while, no one spoke.

Then Eris whispered, "We're not alone anymore."

That night, they gathered on the bluff for the first Night of Telling. It wasn't planned — it simply happened, as such nights often do.

Evara began with Kaedon's story — how the man of shadow and light had sung a door open through the dying sun. Danea followed with her mother's forge hymn, a deep, rhythmic chant that made the fire itself seem to sway.

Tahlia told of Lumera's last experiment, how a single mirror caught enough light to project a map of memory, a promise that wherever the sun went, their story followed.

Then Lira, the youngest, spoke.

Her voice trembled, but every head turned toward her.

"My grandmother said," Lira began, "that every light carries memory. If that's true, then we brought all of them here. Maybe they're looking at us now — all the people who couldn't come. Maybe they're in the second sun, smiling. So tonight, when you look up, don't see stars. See faces."

Silence followed. Not empty, but full, full of all the names that lived inside them still.

When the fire died down, Eris stepped away from the circle, climbing higher on the bluff until she could see the bay shimmer under the new constellations. Somewhere in that sky, a faint thread of gold pulsed, the Sky River, still glowing faintly with the echo of Aurethis's light.

She thought of Sera, of Lumera, of Kaedon, of the millions left behind.

And she whispered, not as a prayer, but as a declaration:

"We remember. And we continue."

The next dawn broke clean and radiant.

Above the bay, the Veyra descended through thin clouds, trailing light like a comet returning home.

The settlers lifted their faces and cheered.

Children ran, shouting, as dust rose in golden swirls.

Nivara stepped down the ramp first, followed by Tavir, his cloak bright with static, eyes wet but smiling. He looked around — at the hills, the river, the gathered people, and the animals grazing near the edge of the field — and said simply:

"We made it. All of us."

And the crowd answered as one voice carried by wind and memory:

"Welcome home."

That night, from the highest tower of Promise Bend, a tower built from the bones of three ships and the courage of hundreds, Nivara recorded the first formal message of the New Alliance of Illumeris:

"To any who come after: We were not gods. We were the frightened children of a dying sun. But we remembered how to build, how to sing, and how to forgive. We have named this place Illumeris after the light we followed. We hope you find us. Or, if not, we hope you build your own dawn."

She sealed the message inside a glass capsule, to be placed at the base of the tower. A simple inscription was carved into the metal beneath it:

For those who dared to carry the sun.

And far above, beyond even the reach of Illumeris's new orbit, something unseen flickered, a final reflection from the dying world of Aurethis, sending its last light across the dark to find them.

It took centuries for that light to arrive.

But when it did, the people of Illumeris saw the heavens blaze gold one more time, and they knew, without question, that their home had said goodbye.

CHAPTER 15

The Legacy

The map of Promise Bend no longer fit on a single page. It wrapped the inside walls of the Hall of Wind and Memory, an evolving mural painted on glass and storm cloth, its coastline updated every solstice, its rivers traced in copper thread that darkened with the oils of any hand that lingered too long. New settlements budded beyond the first bluff like punctuation added by a confident writer: Harbour of Quiet Tides, Reedstone, Mirrorfield, Kite's Rest. Far inland, faint lines marked caravan routes that had begun as questions and hardened into roads.

None of it would have surprised the first one thousand.

All of it would have filled them, in equal measure, with joy and warning.

On Founders' Day, the day the sky burned ceremonial gold with luminescent kites, and the river wore a necklace of boats, the Hall opened its doors to anyone who wished to remember.

Nael Vareth-Sael, a scholar of the Archive at twenty-one cycles and a child of two traditions that once preferred to admire each other at arm's length, stood before the mural and tilted her head.

Her hair, pale as wind-polished reed, was braided in the Varethine manner but threaded with copper wire, a Solenari habit so that when she moved, the braid clicked softly like a small machine learning to purr. She traced the coastline with her eyes, not her fingers; the archivist's first oath was to leave a first surface untouched.

Behind her, the Hall breathed with a hundred small sounds that had become as local as weather: the whistle of a kettle in the teaching alcove, the whirr of a wind harp tuning itself, the soft scuff of boots respectful of polished glass.

"Your grandmother would say we've made a mess," Mira Kelen said, stepping to Nael's side with the lazy grace of a poet whose notebooks had become school texts against her will.

She was greyer now, joyfully so, her words both bolder and more careful.

Nael smiled. "My grandmother would ask whether the mess sings."

Mira's eyes brightened. "Does it?"

Nael tilted her head in that half-listening way the Varethine were famous for and the Aerethi claimed to have invented first.

She heard the city outside making its daily argument in the voice of work, hammers flattering glass into shape, children reciting names during the morning telling, water bragging quietly about being river and not sea. "It's a harmony," she decided. "But we've started leaning on the top voice. Expansion is louder than memory."

"That's what you're speaking about today?" Mira asked. "At the Hall?"

Nael glanced at the sun through the skylight.

The light here was a quieter cousin to the old Aurethis glare, soft honey over steel instead of a welding arc, and she loved it for that gentleness and resented it for the reminders it did not carry. "That," she said, "and a story I'm not supposed to know."

"Oh?"

"The one in the sealed spindle. The one Lynis left hidden in a listening-stone under the Crossroads dais. The one that only hums when you sing the cadence backward." Nael said, trying not to sound like someone who had broken into her own history and only regretted the door hinge.

Mira raised an eyebrow. "I always suspected the child of a Vareth and a Solenari would refuse to keep secrets in the right direction."

Nael grinned. "We inherit disobedience as naturally as eye colour."

"And the spindle?" Mira asked, but she didn't press; poets prefer to be shown, not told.

"In the address," Nael said softly, "Kaedon says something we did not record the first time. He says: If you make it, build schools first. Not for knowledge, for listening."

Mira sighed, the sound of a long-held certainty finally given permission to sit. "Then let's go listen."

They crossed the square.

Founders' Day blew warm off the bay.

Kites glittered like fish scouting the aerial tide. The tall, gentle animals from the first days, now simply called lattice-backs, grazed at the river's bend, their fronds catching light and throwing it casually back at the crowd as if to say, Yes, yes, we are still magnificent; please carry on.

Children ran with backpacks shaped like the first Arks, the way children everywhere turn catastrophe into costume.

At the centre of Promise Bend stood the Pillars of the Four, carved from ship spar and fossilised reed, their surfaces inlaid with images: Lumera bent over a lattice of light that looked like music frozen mid-gesture; Sera, her hand on a conduit, laughter cut into the grain; Tavir leaning into wind as if it could lean back; Kaedon half-turned toward a doorway he had already entered. Around the base lay the Hundred Stones—river-smoothed markers etched with the names of those first chosen from each culture. Families came here when they wanted to remember what the word, we had cost them and what it had bought.

Nael paused, resting two fingers lightly on Stone 87: Mira Kelen, Poet.

"I didn't know they carved me so soon," Mira said, amused and a little annoyed. "I'm not done."

"None of these are finished," Nael said. "That's the point."

The Hall of Telling had been built with hill-light and water-dark in mind. Sun perforated its ceiling through mirror-vents cut in Solenari geometry; shadow pooled in the floor's low basins, Varethine style, so words could cool before they were believed. On one side, Aerethi vanes turned with the slightest draft, revealing wind to the eye; on the other, a Thalanor heat-well breathed the slow, constant warmth of an argument you leave on the back burner because it burns best when you let it.

The room had filled long before Nael arrived.

Eris Thal sat near the back, boots off, legs comfortably crossed, a bandage on one hand where a new solar rig had refused to accept advice.

Karo, her cousin, stood near the door, whispering to a crowd of apprentices in whom the future lay complaining and hopeful.

Ryn Kelen leaned against a pillar with the practiced casualness of a man who had aged into wisdom after skidding through several near misses.

Tahlia, hair silvered at the temples but eyes unchanged, held a slate and whispered time cues to the one official the Alliance had bothered to elect: Liora, a quiet administrator whose superpower was making sure nothing important got lost between people who loved each other enough to argue constantly.

Nael climbed the dais.

She did not stand behind the lectern.

She stood on the edge, feet almost over the drop, because she believed some truths behave better when spoken without furniture.

"Founders," she began, and the room hushed not because of a title but because the word had an echo; it included so many absent ears. "We tell our beginning like a song because it is one. We sing the cadence and pretend we understand it. But cadence without listening becomes a march, and I've yet to see a march build a kitchen."

Soft laughter cooled the room.

"We've added cities to the map," Nael continued.

"We've tamed kites that once dragged us across the sand. We've convinced the sky that we mean to stay, and so far, it has not corrected us. But I have been listening to a voice we put in a box for safekeeping. You know it."

She lifted a thin crystal sealed in old cloth. Half the room exhaled as if she had brought a ghost. "The spindle Lynis left under the Crossroads. It contains a last note, a request."

She set it in the song cradle at the dais' edge. She did not call for silence; she called for softness. The room's acoustics shifted; the wind vanes slowed; the heat-well breathed just enough to keep hands from finding each other only because of the cold.

Nael sang the cadence backward.

The first sound was unfamiliar and disagreeable, like a polite refusal. Then the spindle woke and gave back the old man's voice.

"If you make it," Kaedon said, thin as if spoken through time's-tired throat, "build schools first. Not for knowledge. For listening. You have learned to cross distances. Learn to bridge differences. This one is harder. Ask your children what the wind said to their grandparents and what their grandparents misheard."

He laughed, and the room laughed with him, generations late and right on time.

"Teach them a thing we did badly: to argue while holding hands. Teach them to be more curious than correct. Teach them to make a seat for grief at the table and pour it water. I will not arrive where you are. That is good. Elders ruin new rooms by rearranging furniture. Go make rooms I would not recognise."

Silence pooled in the basins; the vanes made three slow turns.

Nael touched the spindle off. She didn't fill the gap. She let the room breathe.

Then she said: "So today we add a new vow to Founders' Day. We will build eight schools in eight quarters—one in Promise Bend; one at the Harbour; one at the reed lakes; one at the northern ridge; one on the islands; one at Mirrorfield; one where the caravans pass, not stop; and one that will move with the wind. Their curriculum is simple: first listening, then making, then correction. Not the other way around."

Murmurs.

Approving.

Puzzled.

Irritated.

Relieved.

The right mix for a town still alive enough to mistrust simple answers.

A hand rose.

Grand Marshal Seret, the closest thing Promise Bend had to a keeper of edges. Her uniform dusted with reed pollen because she refused to separate her authority from places where flowers grew.

"What of the expansion proposals?" she asked. "We've petitions for three more inland settlements and a sky-tether experiment at Kite's Rest. And the breeders want permission to shape the lattice-backs for load-bearing work."

The room cooled further.

Nael glanced at Eris, who made a face that meant, to say it out loud, or I will.

"Everything we add," Nael said, "we also agree to listen to. Expansion that does not listen is extraction. We did not come here to mine a planet for bragging rights. The lattice-backs stepped in our prints the first day to say we would be watched while we watched. We will not put a harness on the creature that taught us how to walk softly."

Eris whooped before she remembered she was old enough to pretend restraint; the room laughed and knocked hands on benches in the old Thalanor applause. Ryn rolled his eyes with affection. Tahlia wrote something down that had the shape of a policy.

"Sky-tether?" Seret persisted.

"Test it over water," Nael said promptly. "With four release points and a council of pilots who've flown into thunder and back. The tether is a story we tell gravity; we should begin with politeness."

Mira murmured, "Remind me to write that on a door."

Liora raised a hand, but not to speak; to ask the room to listen again.

"Let's cast it," she said. "A vote is a kind of listening; it asks our differences to be brave."

They cast bits of glass into bowls.

As always, one for Yes, one for No, one for Not-Yet. The Not-Yet bowl had saved more friendships than any law.

When the last shard rang against its chosen echo, Liora tipped the bowls onto cloths.

Schools: Yes, with Not-Yet from those anxious about taking cooks from kitchens and pilots from towers.

Sky-tether: Not-Yet, testing required.

Lattice-back harnesses: No, with a handful of Yes shards glinting like stubbornness under a clear stream.

"Good," Mira murmured, and wrote a single line on her palm to finish later:

We became a people by learning where not to put our hands.

Founders' Day spills into night the way the river spills into the bay—inevitably, with grace, and occasionally with slight accidents involving wine.

At the Four Flame Trees, grown from cuttings carried painfully across the sky and coaxed into the soil with songs that embarrassed engineers and delighted children.

The elders lit the first lanterns.

Each lantern was inscribed with the name of someone who had not crossed or had crossed and not arrived.

They were set on the river to teach water to remember us, the way Kaedon insisted it could.

Eris found Karo where the lanterns caught on a slow eddy. He had a new burn on his wrist and new patience with his mouth.

"You argued well this morning," she said.

"I'm learning with age," he replied. "Yours."

She shouldered him amicably. "Send that joke into the river; it will corrode."

He nodded toward the bluff.

"They're bringing the First Ledger."

Eris looked up.

Nael and Liora were carrying a glass-and-leather book cradled like a child. Mira followed, hand on the frame as if steadying her own words.

Behind them came a long line of citizens: a midwife with tired joy stamped around her eyes; a pilot with cloud-salt dried in his hair; a baker who smelled like refuge; three children with faces painted as lattice-backs because that's what courage looked like this year.

The Ledger was set on a low table near the flame roots.

Its first page, the one written on Night One, was faded soft from a century of fingertips.

New pages waited.

Liora turned three at once: one marked Births, one Deaths, and one Promises.

Nael, hands steady as ritual, read last year's promises aloud:

We promised to speak one truth gently every day.

We promised to waste no morning.

We promised to ask forgiveness of the ground when we forgot to look where we put our feet.

We promised to teach the cadence to every child before their seventh rain.

The crowd answered each line in the old call:

We did mostly.

We tried; the mornings were impatient.

We knelt; the ground forgave, which is not the same as forgetting.

We taught the children and corrected our rhythm.

Laughter and throat-thick swallowing braided into something edible.

"New promises?" Liora asked.

A small hand lifted. Jace Thal-Vareth, eight years sun-counted, hair refusing to submit to any comb, eyes serious like long tunnels. "Can we promise not to call it our planet?" he asked. "Because it isn't. It's itself."

Silence, then a murmuring as the idea found room. Liora smiled as if she had been waiting for someone to give permission to a thought she'd been carrying like a sleeping bird.

"Yes," she said. "We can promise that."

Mira wrote quickly:

We promise to call Illumeris by its name more often than by ours.

Another hand, Lira Sael, grown now, her drawings of wind collected like scripture by engineers who didn't admit they read poetry.

"We promise to keep a small place in every house for grief."

No one needed to ask why.

The river was already lit with lanterns.

A third hand. This time it was Seret.

"We promise to teach the old warnings with the new joys. Expansion and listening, as the scholar said."

Eris lifted her hand, then lowered it.

She didn't need to add anything. Sometimes the truest oversight is to stop overseeing and start watching.

When the last promise was inked, Liora turned the page and wrote the date, which they now counted two ways: Year 104 After Crossing / Year 1 of the Listening Schools. She signed with a flourish that belonged to a pragmatist, then closed the Ledger as if closing an eye that had just seen something beloved.

A wind moved across the crowd the type of wind that lifts hair and settles hearts. From the bluff, Nivara whistled the old Aerethi call, and kites groaned pleasantly on their lines as if waking.

Then the choirs, no longer merely Solenari but several hundred voices trained to hold mirrors quiet and hold grief calmer, began the Cadence of Remembrance.

Not the one that opened doors, the one that let a room be a room where those who had left could sit unseen without making the living polite to the point of silence.

Three bright.

The lanterns flared.

Pause.

The crowd breathed together.

Two dim.

The river darkened to allow the sky to show off a little.

Long silence.

It held.

No one forced it to end.

Five.

Children smiled at each other because they were counting and winning.

The flame trees hummed in their slow, wooden way. On the far bank, lattice-backs lifted their heads and swung their fronds in time, as if remembering a gene-deep rehearsal.

"Schools first," Mira whispered, and squeezed Nael's hand.

"Listening first," Nael corrected softly, and Mira squeezed harder.

Later, when the sisters of the night had traded the loud work for the quiet, Nael climbed the Crossroads — no longer a bare ring but a gardened geometry.

Solenari prism-flowers caught dew and separated it into colour; Varethine pools held stars the sky hadn't assigned yet; Aerethi vanes whispered weather gossip to anyone awake enough to eavesdrop; Thalanor heat vents breathed steadily, warming the roots of trees that had consented to a bargain with stone.

She placed the sealed spindle back in its cavity beneath the dais.

It resisted at first, then slid home with a sound like agreement.

"Thank you," she said to no one in particular and everyone who had taught her to be particular about gratitude.

A presence moved in the shadow line.

Evara stepped from behind a pillar, walking stick tapping lightly.

"You could have scolded me for opening it," Nael said without turning.

"I could have," Evara agreed. "But then who would have taught me the backward song?"

Nael smiled at the near-elder beside her.

Evara's hair was a cloud of white now, her face cut with kindness, her eyes as stern as when she'd first shepherded truth through a door guarded by men afraid of the cost of being right.

"Do you ever miss him?" Nael asked.

"All the time," Evara said.

"And never. Missing is a habit we overfeed. I prefer to practice presence with the absent."

She tapped the dais. "You did well. The old want many things; to be useful to the living is most of them."

They stood for a while, listening to the Crossroads breathe.

Finally, Nael said, "Will we ever open the river again? Not just for ships. For messages. For love."

Evara laughed, delighted by the audacity disguised as research. "Oh, child. We never closed it. We just learned not to shout."

She lifted her stick and traced a shallow curve in the dew on the dais—two spirals, interlocking. "Carry this into the schools," she said. "Teach them it's not two worlds we balance, but two ways of paying attention. Then tell me when you're done. I will want to argue."

"While holding hands," Nael said.

"While holding hands," Evara echoed.

They left the Crossroads to the night, which made a better archivist than any human on good days.

Over Promise Bend, the kites rode the late wind; on the river, lanterns drifted like unhurried thoughts.

In the grass, a child slept on a blanket patterned with the old sun and the new, dreaming of names not yet needed.

And Illumeris, which was itself and in no danger of being ours, listened.

The world remembered the four who had carried it this far, light, shadow, wind, and flame, and the many who had agreed to carry the rest. The promise had already changed shape, as promises must when they're kept.

In the morning, under the first bell, a boy would run through the schoolyard and shout with the proud tyranny of youth, "Teacher says listening is homework!"

And a girl would answer, hands on hips, "Good. Then we're finally doing the hard part."

The wind would add a note.

The trees would adjust the harmony.

Deep somewhere beneath the Crossroads, the echo of an old man's laugh would find its shelf in the new library and stay a while.

CHAPTER 16

The Tether and the Tide

The first time the sky-tether rose over Promise Bend, people stepped outside without meaning to.

Doors swung open in unison. Ladles paused mid-soup. A lattice-back on the far bank lifted its head and rotated every frond until it shimmered like a polite question.

The tether gleamed—a thread so fine it seemed spun from the hush itself.

It climbed from an anchored platform out in the bay and ran to four release pylons spaced along the curve of water, each pylon built low and broad so no single failure would become a story without an ending. The line's heart was storm glass braided with hollow reed and a filament of Solenari metal the colour of dew; it could sing stress before it snapped and, if persuaded with the correct chord, would forget to transmit shock.

Nael Vareth-Sael stood at the end of Pylon East, hair wrapped in a kerchief the colour of mirror-copper, notebook tucked under one arm, a coil of listening wire around her wrist.

At her shoulder, Mira Kelen hummed a scale to the wind.

"It should be over water," Mira murmured, not for the first time.

"It is," Nael replied, also not for the first time. "And over ethics."

Mira smiled sidelong. "You enjoy this part too much."

"It's the only part that resists being graded." Nael gestured at the floating platform, a disk of welded hull plates and timber, anchored by Thalanor conduits that drank heat from a shallow vent below. "We lift the test car five spans, then ten. We monitor strain with song, not just gauges. We let the sea say something about our ambition."

"And if the sea says 'no'?"

"Then we thank it for the answer." Nael tapped her coil. "And write a better question."

She could feel the bay through the wire. The slow, back-and-forth grammar of tide, the small shoulders of chop, the way the river offered, and the ocean edited. The tether's hum slid under all of it: tentative, proud, the voice of a device new to its body.

"Ready on West," Karo Thal crackled over the wind-comm.

"Ready on South," answered Seret, whose reluctant endorsement had chaperoned this experiment from rumour to scaffolding.

"Ready on North," Ryn Kelen said, clipped and calm, as if giving the wind a chance to disagree.

"Ready at Platform," came Eris Thal, breath bright, impatience disciplined. "Pilot council in position. Test car secured. She wants to fly."

"Wants," Mira murmured. "We used to burn worlds by mistaking that word."

Nael looked down the line.

Children from the Listening School had gathered at each pylon with teachers, clipboards, and the fierce seriousness of young beings entrusted with adult work. At Pylon East, Jace Thal-Vareth was checking knots with the slow dignity of an eight-year-old who still measured his life by rains and kites.

Two older pupils, Amra and Dell, cupped their ears to reed-horns aimed at the storm glass line, translating tension into pitch.

Nael crouched to Jace's height. "You call it out if the note climbs too fast."

He nodded. "The line says 'quiet-quiet-louder.' If it says 'loud-loud-snap,' I will use my big voice."

"What is the rule?" Amra prompted the younger boy.

"Listening first. Then the making. Then correction," Jace recited, squeezing each word into a neat shape, too aware that Mira was nearby and might put him in a poem without consent.

Nael rose, met Mira's eye. The poet's grin softened into pride.

Across the bay, the platform's winches hummed. The tether trembled, a low purr that turned the skin to air. The test car, little more than a compact basket of ballast with a wind-tail and a quilt of sensors stitched to its flank, rose one span, then two. Spray glittered from its ribs as it climbed through sea-breath into sky-breath.

"Five spans," Eris reported. "Holding at five."

Nael listened. The line sang amber and honey. The pylons replied with a satisfied chord. The sound of materials remembering what they were made for.

"Ten," Eris called. "Holding at ten."

The tether brightened along its length as sunlight found the braided reed and Solenari thread. Lattice-backs on the far bank shifted to face it fully, as if a new plant had unfurled in their field of notice. Children at the pylons took turns laying palms to the bases, learning heat and strain the way the Thalanor had taught them—by touch first.

"Fifteen," Eris said. "Wind shifts north-northeast. Correcting with a vane."

A gust combed the bay, laying a hand across the platform's shoulder. The test car wobbled; the song climbed half a note then settled.

"Praise your grandmothers," murmured Mira.

"Always," Nael said.

"Twenty."

On the bluff above Promise Bend, Nivara stood with arms folded, gaze narrowed to the colour of caution. Tahlia beside her scrolled through wind data, mapping the invisible for those who still preferred their truths diagrammed. Liora had stationed herself at the first-aid canopy without fuss about position—Administration, to her, meant standing where the panic was most likely to congregate and then talking it into something useful.

The car held at twenty spans.

The tether's hum found a pleasing groove. Nael exhaled the breath she had been storing since dawn.

"Bring her down," she said into the comm, and the platform's winches obliged. Twenty became fifteen, ten, five. Water accepted the test car back with a splash that sounded like applause.

The bay people cheered.

Someone on the platforms banged a pan with a wrench, which in Promise Bend meant certainty of dinner.

"Phase One successful," Seret announced.

The old soldier rarely smiled on duty. She did now, privately, as if admitting pleasure could be tactically disastrous.

Nael should have written that very sentence, dated and clean, into the Hall's ledger and left the day to ripen untroubled. But the sky is a co-author. It reflexed a muscle no one had checked that morning.

The tide ran early.

At first, it looked like impatience—chop sharpening, foam lifting where it usually rubbed. Then the river's mouth narrowed under a force it didn't invite. The platform rode a swell that didn't belong to the bay.

Nivara's head snapped toward the horizon. "Tahlia?"

Tahlia's fingers flew. "Barometric drop offshore. Not enough for a storm. It's... a set of long-period waves. Deep-water push. Source unknown."

"Volcanic shelf?" Ryn guessed over the comm.

"Not within our map radius," Tahlia said. "And it feels too regular, too practiced."

The first long wave rolled beneath the platform, lifting it like a parent with a sullen child.

It wasn't large.

It was insistent.

The tether swayed in a slow arc and sang a note no one had taught it.

Amra flinched. "Teacher?"

Nael crouched between the pupils, pressing the reed-horn to her own ear.

The pitch was not panic yet.

It was an argument.

"Four-release protocol," Nael said into the comm. "Prepare on my count. We'll unhook in sequence and let the car run as a kite to bleed tension."

"Copy," Seret and Ryn said together, voices braiding like old rope.

On the platform, Eris swore with affection. "She was just starting to like me."

"Listen before you soothe," Nael said. "Count of five. North, then East, then West, then South. Ready?"

"Ready."

"Three bright. Pause. Two dim. Long silence. Five," Nael counted, turning the cadence into coordination.

Pylon North's latch sang open; the line snapped once and settled. East's latch followed—Nael felt it through the base more than heard it, a relief that ran up her calves and told her exactly how heavy the water had just become. West. South. The test car lifted as the tether freed the platform from geometric obligations, and for a moment the sky pretended it was easy to get along with physics.

Then the second pulse hit.

It came low and heavy, shouldering into the river mouth without asking directions. The platform rode it without grace; the test car dipped, then recovered; the tether swung across the bay in a long glittering curve and cut a shadow across sunlit water.

At Pylon East, Jace pointed. "Fish!"

Dozens, no, hundreds of small, silver-bodied creatures skittered across the surface in a spray of suicidal joy, then dove all at once in a pattern too synchronised to be panic.

Farther out, something larger broke water.

Sleek, dark, curious and then slid under, as if endorsing the wave.

"Not a storm," Amra said softly. "Migration."

Nael felt the note beneath what her eyes brought—a rhythm too regular for accident. "The tether is standing across a path," she realised aloud. "We are a clothesline in a street."

She pressed the comm. "Hold the car in the north carve. Let the line drift high. Give anything that needs to pass room and a shadow to aim for."

Eris had already started the manoeuvre. The test car obeyed the wind with gratitude; the tether settled into a catenary that looked like a smile repaired after an argument.

On the bluff, Nivara exhaled. "Well done."

"Not done," Tahlia murmured, eyes narrowing again— this time not in caution but curiosity. The second long wave drew the river higher into the harbour's curve than usual, lapping at the low steps near the market. People moved goods without panic but with the energy of anyone suddenly reminded that nature didn't sign their schedules.

"Seret," Liora called through the admin channel, "begin high-move protocol in the lower market. Not evacuation. Elevation. We'll stack, not scatter. Kitchens first."

Seret's teams flowed into lanes like ink finding its letter. The Listening School bell rang.

Not alarm but assembly.

Students grabbed reed-horns, mirror-plates, and chalk.

This was what they'd trained for: translating a world's mood into action without insulting it by yelling.

At Pylon East, Nael's pupils stood taller; even Jace's big voice found itself unnecessary. If there's a better education than seeing your study turn into usefulness without your panic, Nael hadn't met it.

The third pulse came with a gift and a demand.

Gift: the shallow reed lagoons filled enough for the nursery fish to push upriver, where they would lay ribbons of eggs among the stalks. Demand: the current pinched into the bend near the Four Flame Trees, undercutting the bluff below the Pillars of the Four.

Mira saw it first. "Roots," she said, and took off running with an energy that mocked joints which had politely asked to be consulted.

Nael was right behind her. The base of the bluff had been reinforced generations ago with glass-rock and woven reed. It had held admirably against rain and time. It did not like surges that came from the side rather than above.

At the tree line, Eris arrived from the platform at the same heartbeat as Karo from Pylon West and Ryn from North. They met without explaining how people with a life of shared emergencies always meet, each seeing different parts of the same whole.

"Not a collapse," Eris said, one hand on a Flame Tree's warm trunk, eyes on the undercut where water chewed at the bluff. "A correction," she amended. "If we let it speak."

"We could drop rip-cribs," Karo suggested, already unrolling coils of bio-wire from a carry bag.

"Over water," Nael said. "With four release points. And we ask the river where it wants the crib, not where we think it will look nice."

Ryn shaded his eyes to find the surface vector.

"We station the lattice-backs as visual markers. They stand where the ground is most certain; their weight distribution reads better than our sensors in shallows."

Mira laughed, breathless. "I waited sixty years to hear an engineer say that sentence."

Ryn shrugged. "We grew up."

Seret's runners arrived with woven crib frames, children from the school bearing handfuls of living reed for anchoring. Liora directed traffic with the tone of a person who has kept soup from boiling over during a thunderstorm while three dignitaries argued about soup.

Nael turned to the students. "What do we ask first?"

"Where are we wrong?" Dell recited.

"And second?"

"What do you need from us?" Amra said, not to Nael but to the river.

The children knelt and pushed mirror-plates into the water at arm's length. On each plate was etched the simplest grid. They watched how ripples crossed it, how the grid bowed, how light tore and mended. Jace lay full-length and put his ear to the ground, learning with bone.

"Here," he said, astonished by his own certainty, pointing ten paces downstream from the undercut. "It's hungry there and tired here."

"Tired is where we build," Nael said. "Hungry is where we feed."

They set the first crib at Tired. It settled with a burp of gratitude, reeds spearing mud with the alacrity of beings who enjoy new work.

They set the second at Hungry, but with its slatted face open, not closing. The river could lick, not bite, and leave something of itself to grow. Two more cribs went in on Nael's count, positioned to braid the flow back into the middle instead of letting it gnaw the bank.

The fourth wave rolled through like a big laugh that had found its volume. The cribs flexed and held. The undercut darkened but stopped growing. Above, the roots of the Flame Trees relaxed into their purchase on the bluff.

"Good," Nivara said, not by comm but by presence; she had come down the path, hands dirty, hair blown to argument. She squeezed Nael's shoulder, then Karo's, then Ryn's, without ceremony. "Now do it again for the market steps."

They did.

By afternoon, the tide had learned a new way to enter Promise Bend.

The first nursery fish surged into reeds they found surprisingly ready. Children marked spawning clusters on slates, then ran messages to the baker because life is nothing if you don't eat after you work.

As the water gentled and the tether's song settled back into contentment, the pilot council met under an awning to write what had just happened into policy. Not because writing made it true, but because free memory is impolite to the future.

"Rule One," Seret said, holding chalk like a weapon she had sheathed. "Tether operations are suspended during long-wave events. Definition: any pulse that moves the market steps three or more risers."

"Rule Two," Ryn added. "Tether height defaults to migration catenary under long-period oscillations. We do not stand across streets."

"Rule Three," Nael said, "Schools co-lead observation. No flight if children cannot translate the notes."

Mira underlined that one twice, then drew a tiny ear beside it.

"Rule Four," Eris said, eyes far on the horizon where the fresh waves had come from. "We ask what sent the push. If it's wind over deep, we note the season. If it's moon tug—" She broke off, amused. "We don't have a name for this moon yet."

"We ask it first," Nivara said dryly. "Before naming things after ourselves."

"Rule Five," Liora said, pencil already moving over a clean page in the Ledger. "All rules may be argued; none may be ignored."

"Rule Six," Jace piped up from the corner, sticky with reed-sap and triumph. "If you hear loud-loud-snap, you use your big voice."

"Unanimous," Mira said, banging a spoon on a cup.

They laughed—not hard, not long, but with the relief of people who had learned again the particular calm that follows correct listening.

At dusk, the tether glowed like a vein under skin; wind-kites hung from the bluff, idling in a sky that had decided to be forgiving.

The Four Flame Trees shed a few leaves.

Not from stress, from opinion and the river smoothed itself under the new crib geometry as if adjusting a sleeve.

The Hall of Telling filled without invitation. You'd think a town would be tired after such a day; you'd be wrong. Fatigue often remembers how to be joy if you feed it bread and give it to someone else's story to hold for a while.

Nael stepped onto the dais with wet cuffs and reed cuts on her fingers. She looked less like a scholar than a fisher who'd been caught by the net she meant to cast. Good. The schools would approve.

"We tried to touch the sky today," she said, voice hoarse but steady. "It touched back, and so did the sea. We learned a thing we all suspected: the world has routes we did not pave. Our tether will require permission from fish, waves, and a creature that stepped in our prints to show us how to walk. We will continue the experiment over water, not land. We will write our questions in chorus. And when the tide speaks early, we will not call it rude."

Murmurs.

Agreement running like a quiet current.

A few scowls from those who smelled delay and thought it the same as failure.

That was all right.

A town without impatience grows lazy.

"Listening report?" Liora prompted, and three students trooped up with reed-horns and mirror plates. Amra spoke for them without snatching credit.

"The line's note climbs sooner near the river's mouth than near the harbour's curve," she said. "That means questions like, 'Do we lift at the mouth and anchor at the curve?' Also, the fish like to run in shadow. The tether's shadow helped them choose. That's not a reason to keep it low; it's a reminder to learn shadow as a tool, not an accident."

Dell held up a chalkboard diagram of the cribs and the new flow pattern. He had drawn the river as a person, which is the sort of sin engineers forgive if the math follows. "Hungry here, tired here. We fed the hungry, supported the tired, and the river said, 'thank you' by not eating our library."

Jace stepped up last, unexpectedly solemn. "The tree said, 'Hold,'" he reported. "Not with my ear. With my back." Children do this sometimes—translate sensation into vocabulary that makes adults sit down. Several did. Mira wrote furiously on a scrap of sail.

Nael kissed each child's forehead. This is how a community certifies its own scientists—no medals, just contact with a head that worked hard in good faith.

From the back, Eris lifted a cup. "To the tide for being our teacher," she called.

The room echoed it: "To the tide!"

"To the tether for being humble," Ryn added.

"To the children for telling us when to shut up," Mira said, which got the loudest laugh and the most honest applause.

They ate. They sang—not the door-opening cadence, but the stillness song that keeps mirrors from catching what must be released. Afterward, as lanterns formed a fresh constellation on the river, Nael, and Mira climbed the bluff. The sky was freckled with stars Illumeris had worn long before they arrived and would keep wearing whether or not humans learned to deserve beauty.

"You were right," Mira said at last. "Over water."

"You were right," Nael answered. "Over ethics."

"We're not done," Mira added, as if either of them had suggested rest.

"We've never been done," Nael said. "We've only been interrupted by survival."

The tether hummed, low and pleased, a dog at its master's heel that had learned the command stay and enjoyed obeying when the game made sense. The river slid by with the confidence of an old runner who had found his pace again. The Flame Trees sighed, as if grateful for the excuse to show their roots to the sun and be thanked for it.

An anonymous hand that might have been Amra's, Dell's, Jace's, or had chalked down below, in the schoolyard on the wall the winds:

LESSON 1: ASK.

LESSON 2: ASK BETTER.

LESSON 3: WHEN WATER ANSWERS, CHANGE
THE PLAN.

Mira nudged Nael's shoulder. "You'll take this to the inland schools?"

"I will," Nael said. "And I'll tell them the tether is not a ladder to heaven. It's a handshake with the weather. If you squeeze too hard, you lose the friend."

"Write that down," Mira said, and then, because poets are the honest thieves of history, "I already have."

They stood until the sky thinned toward sleep. Somewhere out beyond the reef, long waves kept moving, reminding the bay that distances have conversations too. Up the river, in reed-beds newly decorated with eggs, tiny silver lives argued themselves into the future. On the far bank, lattice-backs bedded down, fronds folded just-so to shed dew onto roots.

And in the Hall of Telling, Liora closed the Ledger on a day that had started with ambition and ended with a blueprint for humility. She wrote one more line under Promises before snapping the leather strap:

We promise to let the world interrupt us.

When morning came, the plans were lighter on paper and stronger in mind. The tether team ate early and walked to the pylons without a parade. The school bells rang, a listening bell first and a work bell second. The tide, having delivered its message, went about the business of holding up the world.

On the platform, Eris patted the winch housing. "Round two," she told it. "No heroics. Our grandchildren need boring legends."

Nael tied her coil of wire, then paused and pressed palm to pylon, ear to reed-horn. The note was friendly. The day, for now, consented to being ordinary.

But in Promise Bend, ordinary had learned another word: attentive.

And attentive, they had decided, was how you built a civilization without breaking the planet that was kind enough to hold your weight.

CHAPTER 17

The Sky That Learned Their Names

The third year of the Listening Schools began beneath a sky that seemed to know their schedules. It arrived on time, blue, curious, a little shy about the attention.

The wind carried the scent of wet sand and the low hum of confidence that came when human activity stopped threatening to break rhythm and started joining it.

Promise Bend had become less of a settlement and more of a symphony.

The flame trees at the bluff's edge shaded the Hall of Telling with crimson-gold fronds; the bay glittered with tether pylons that gleamed at dawn and whispered at dusk. Between them lay a town that thought in conversations: glassworkers who sang to sand until it cooled in agreement, farmers who negotiated with soil, children who apologised to puddles when they stepped too hard.

And yet, beyond the gentle hum of creation, a new restlessness grew—one shaped like wings.

Nael heard it first from Eris Thal, who arrived at her office in the Listening School with eyes as bright as trouble disguised as curiosity.

"They've done it," Eris said. "The Sky Federation has approved the tether-lift trials."

Nael set down her stylus. "I thought the Federation disbanded after the Ark years."

"They did," Eris said. "But their grandchildren didn't. Ryn's boy and Nivara's niece—they've formed a council up north. They call themselves the Wind Pilots of Illumeris. They want to use the tether as the base for a vertical migration system."

Nael blinked. "Migration? We've just learned to stay put."

Eris grinned. "Apparently, staying put offends some families' sense of adventure."

That night, the Wind Pilots arrived.

They came not in ships but in sleek gliders stitched from storm glass and living reed. They circled over Promise Bend like memories trying to find a place to land. Their leader, a tall woman with copper eyes and a braid full of wind charms, touched down first and bowed low before the Hall of Telling.

"Commander Sela Ryn-Kelen," she said, voice smooth and direct. "Daughter of Ryn, granddaughter of Tavir. We've come to ask permission to speak with the wind."

Nael stood before the assembly. The hall was full—Eris, Mira, Seret, Tahlia, and the council of artisans. Even the lattice-backs had gathered near the windowed walls, their fronds shimmering softly.

Nael studied Sela carefully. "The wind already speaks," she said. "The question is whether you plan to listen."

Sela smiled. "That's the plan, Headmistress. But we believe the upper air holds messages from before the crossing—perhaps echoes of the helix itself. We've built gliders that can follow the old light trails. We want to read what's left behind."

Eris folded her arms. "You're saying the Sky River still exists?"

"Not as a river," Sela replied. "As a residue. Kaedon's cadence might have burned its path into space-time. We think the river's echo touches Illumeris at the edge of its atmosphere, just above the magnetosphere."

Nael frowned. "And you think flying through it will give you... what? History?"

"Maybe," Sela said. "Maybe a way home."

The room stilled. No one had said home that way in years—not as a place they'd left, but as a promise they might still owe.

Mira broke the silence. "If you find Aurethis, what then? The world's dead."

Sela met her gaze. "Perhaps. But dead worlds still dream. We want to know if ours remembers us."

The debate lasted three nights.

Tahlia presented data: wind shear limits, tether strain, temperature thresholds. Ryn—old now, white-haired, fiercely proud—argued that if they denied the young their risks, they'd raise cowards instead of citizens. Liora feared hubris; Seret feared silence if they didn't try. Nael feared neither, but she understood responsibility.

On the fourth dawn, they gathered at the Crossroads Garden. The flame trees shed their petals like falling embers. Nael stood at the centre dais—the same place Lumera Sael had once sung light into glass.

"I have heard your reasoning," she said, "and your fears. I have also listened to the sky. It has not objected. Permission is granted for one ascent. No weapons, no greed, no vanity. Only listening."

Sela bowed. "Understood."

Nael raised her hand. "And one promise. If you find voices in the wind, you must answer them as kin, not conquerors."

The commander nodded. "We are our grandmothers' children. We remember."

The morning of the ascent drew the whole settlement.

The tether gleamed under full sunlight, its braids polished and blessed. At its base, the Wind Pilots prepared their gliders—ten of them, shaped like long, narrow wings with Solenari mirrors running along their spines.

Children painted the hulls with stories: rivers that learned to sing, suns that refused to die, faces of ancestors turned to constellations. The lattice-backs stood at the shore's edge, fronds swaying to a rhythm no one had taught them.

Mira took Nael's hand. "This feels like the old stories again. The kind that starts well and end with a warning."

"All good stories end with warnings," Nael said. "It's how the next ones begin."

At the count of five, the gliders lifted—one after another, catching the tether's updraft and following it skyward. Their wings shimmered gold against the blue. Soon they were dots of light, and then—nothing but bright dust in the air.

"They're gone," Jace whispered.

"Not gone," Eris said. "Learning."

For two days, nothing.

Then, on the third evening, as the sun set red across the bay, the tether hummed.

The note was deep, too low for ears, but the storm glass pylons translated it into vibration. The flame trees trembled. The wind picked up and carried something—soft, rhythmic.

Nael pressed her ear to the pylon. The sound wasn't random. It was a language.

Three bright. Pause. Two dim. Long silence. Five.

The same cadence Kaedon had used to open the sky.

Across the bay, the mirror-pools lit one by one, reflecting not the current sun, but an older, fiercer gold. And in that reflection, for the briefest heartbeat, Nael thought she saw shapes—cities of light, drifting over molten plains. A planet on the edge of death, singing its memory into the void.

Aurethis.

Then the vision faded, leaving only the hum and the shimmer of tears across her reflection.

"They reached it," Mira breathed.

"Or it reached us," Nael whispered.

At dawn, the gliders came back—nine of them.

The tenth was missing.

Sela landed first, her glider scorched at the edges. Her voice cracked as she spoke. "We found the echo. It's not just light—it's patterned energy. The River still flows. It's faint, but alive. We followed it far enough to see fragments—clouds that move like thought, stone that breathes flame."

Nael stepped forward. "And the tenth?"

Sela's eyes filled. "He stayed. Said the current was calling him. He wanted to see the place our ancestors became stars."

No one spoke. Somewhere above them, the sky shimmered faintly gold—as if agreeing.

Eris broke the silence. "Then we send him our thanks. And we make sure he's not alone up there."

That evening, the Hall of Telling filled again. The Wind Pilots reported everything: the resonance patterns, the light fractures, the sound of a voice—faint but unmistakable— woven into the air itself.

Mira asked what it said.

Sela closed her eyes. "It said, we remember you. Keep building."

A murmur went through the hall. Not fear. Reverence.

Nael stood, voice quiet but certain.

"Then we will. We'll build in the wind, as we built on the soil, as we once built from fire and shadow. Not towers, not engines—bridges. Between what was and what will be."

Eris raised her glass. "To the river that never stopped running."

Mira added, "And to the worlds that never stopped listening."

They drank to that—to continuity, to humility, to the brave folly of those who still reached for light even after surviving the dark.

Outside, the tether glowed softly, no longer just an experiment or a device, but a thread of belonging between two suns.

Above it, the stars rearranged themselves slightly, as though making room for a new one, bright and steady, called Illumeris.

And far across the void, on the ghostly plains of Aurethis, a faint pulse answered.

Three bright.

Pause.

Two dim, long silence.

Five.

The rhythm of survival still echoing through light and time.

CHAPTER 18

Bridges of Light

The first blueprint for the orbital listening station did not look like a machine. It looked like a kite. A long-boned diamond with a hollow spine, its skin a patchwork of storm glass, memory-mirror, and reed—materials that had survived the old sun and agreed, cautiously, to serve the new one.

Along its crossbars ran channels for light; along its tail, harmonic vanes that could be tuned by song rather than wrench. In the centre, a throat no wider than a person's shoulders: a chamber where sound could be turned to pattern and pattern to meaning.

They called it the Bridge, not the Station, because the word station suggested standing still, and this device, if it worked, would be the opposite of that—an instrument for crossing without moving, for listening across absence without pretending to own what it heard.

Nael Vareth-Sael held the transparent print to the sun. It scattered thin rainbows over her desk. "It's beautiful," she said, half reluctant. "I don't trust beautiful so quickly."

Across from her, Sela Ryn-Kelen grinned, unrepentant.

"We built gliders, and the sky said yes. We trace the residue of the Sky River, and it returns our calls. The Bridge makes us honest about what we're already doing: answering a voice."

Nael lowered the sheet. "And what if the voice wants quiet?"

"Then we teach the machine to bow," Sela said, as if machinery could learn manners.

Nael looked beyond Sela's shoulder, out at Promise Bend. The town moved like a single organism.

Children running messages, elders chairing arguments, windmills turning without complaint. The tether pylons shone in the morning light. The Four Flame Trees murmured in a low key that meant the roots were satisfied for now.

"Bring it to the Council," Nael said at last. "But bring it as a question, not a foregone conclusion."

Sela thumped her chest lightly, Aerethi salute softened by affection. "I will bring it as a promise to ask better questions."

They convened that afternoon.

Liora, practical as river stones, kept time. Seret stood at the door, not as a guard but as a hinge. Eris Thal arrived with oil on her hands and a burn on her wrist; Ryn with the restlessness of a pilot wearing the ground too long; Tahlia with her slate stacked with winds and numbers. Mira Kelen came last, distracted by a sentence that had been following her all morning and sulking because it refused to be good.

Sela spread the kite-blueprint on the central table.

The glass beneath reflected it twice—once crisp, once slightly delayed.

That delay was accidental in the furniture and intentional in the practice: we do not build as quickly as we admire.

"We anchor the Bridge in the upper thermals," Sela said, tapping the crossbars. "Not a fixed orbit—she breathes with the air, migrates along the sky's slow rivers over weeks. The tail vanes keep the chamber aligned with the resonance layer where the Sky River's echo grazes our magnetosphere."

Ryn leaned in, eyes narrowed. "You'll need a countersong to keep shear from wringing the frame."

Sela smiled. "We'll borrow yours."

Eris squinted at the throat. "Who goes inside?"

"No one," Sela said quickly. "The throat is for instruments only. We learned that much humility during the tether trials."

Mira set her palms on the table. "And what do you plan to hear?"

Sela hesitated. "At first? Harmonic drift. Energy density changes. But Kaedon's cadence wasn't only numbers. It was meaning disguised as rhythm. We believe the Bridge can translate patterned energy into audible code—what you would call speech."

The hall breathed in.

Liora broke the inhale.

"We must ask the other question first: what will it hear from us?"

Tahlia nodded. "If we make a chamber that captures a whisper from the old road, we might become a mouth without intending to. Echoes propagate. The Bridge could speak back just by existing."

"Then we shape the echo," Ryn said. "Tune the chamber to reflect only what we mean to send."

Mira frowned. "Meaning is the one cargo humans never ship honestly."

A murmuring.

Agreement braided with unease.

Eris rolled her bad wrist and winced.

"We built an Ark to leave and were forgiven by history. We built a tether and were corrected by the tide. Now a Bridge. I am not against it. I am against forgetting that tools make habits and habits make ethics lazy."

"Say the laziness," Seret prompted.

Eris sighed. "If the Bridge sings back, and we get used to hearing Aurethis on schedule, who will remember to listen to Illumeris complaining under our feet? The tide will not knock twice to be allowed in."

Nael lifted her hand.

The room quieted the way rooms do when a word is coming that many disagree with, but none will ignore.

"We talk as if Aurethis is our mother and Illumeris our host," she said. "We talk as if the Bridge is an apology for leaving one and a threat to the other. It can be both. Or it can be a third thing: a mirror that refuses to keep what it shows."

She touched the blueprint's throat. "Build it. But bind it. A charter, not just an engine. The Bridge will have laws."

Sela cocked her head.

"What laws does listening require?"

Mira's eyes brightened.

"The good kind. The ones that cost."

They wrote it in the old way: crystal, stone, mouth.

On crystal—thin storm glass slats lashed into a codex—so the sun could read it as it passed. On stone—carved into a slab at the base of the Four Flame Trees, where damp air kept judgment from drying into arrogance. In mouth—memorised by children at the Listening Schools until the words walked without paper.

Article One: Silence first.

The Bridge may only listen for one cycle of moons for every cycle it speaks. If the wind is speechless, it will be too.

Article Two: No summons.

The Bridge may not call to the River without a quorum from the Four Councils.

Light, Shadow, Wind, and Flame and a chorus from the choirs that once calmed mirrors.

We are not owed an answer and will not demand one.

Article Three: Reciprocity.

For every hour spent listening skyward, an equal hour must be spent listening groundward: tide, root, rock, reed, lattice-back. The ledger of this listening will be read publicly each week at the Hall.

Article Four: No single keeper.

The Bridge is stewarded by a braid: a pilot, an engineer, a poet, and a child chosen by lot from the Listening Schools. Any two may halt operations. All four must agree to resume.

Article Five: Unmakeable.

The Bridge must be buildable to be unbuilt. If two Councils call for dismantling, the structure must come apart without needing anyone's death or a miracle.

When they read the Charter aloud in the Hall, the room did not cheer.

It exhaled as if a set of muscles they hadn't noticed were clenching finally loosened. Seret nodded once, satisfied rules had teeth and hands. Ryn, who hated charters on principle, signed it first because he trusted the people holding the pen.

Nael wrote a sixth clause, small, easy to miss, stitched into the margin like a seamstress' joke:

Article Six: When sorrow arrives, seat it.

If communication brings grief, the Bridge will let the town eat together before deciding what to do.

Mira underlined it twice. "Lawful hospitality," she said. "About time."

They built it on the tidal flats, where the river's arguments with the sea made honest ground.

Thalanor welders fused the storm glass ribs with a heat that hummed approval. Solenari glassworkers polished the memory-mirror panels until they remembered without clinging. Varethine scribes etched thin lines of code along the vanes, patterns based on Lynis' backward cadence, so the Bridge would know how to refuse its own temptation to talk too much. Aerethi riggers stitched the reed skin, their knots more poem than rope.

Children ran tools and fetched water and asked questions that made engineers blush in public and edit in private. A lattice-back approached once, sniffed the tail and, satisfied, stepped in the prints of the workers until everyone calmed down enough to laugh.

From the bluff, Nivara watched each phase and said nothing until something was wrong; then she said one word, and everything stopped until it was right.

Tahlia calibrated the harmonic throat with the patience of rivers. Liora kept the ledgers: hours on sky, hours on soil, hours on argument.

After twelve days—because thirteen would have made the superstitious nervous and eleven would have made the conscientious sigh—they walked it to the water like a boat carried to a baptism.

The tether pylons hummed in greeting. The first squall of summer turned the bay silver and then polite again.

"Ready?" Sela asked.

Nael touched the Bridge's vane. "Ask."

They tuned the launch to the stillness song, not the door-opening cadence. The pylons answered. The wind arrived with clean hands.

The Bridge rose, slow as a curtain in a careful play, and found the updraft like a memory finding its shelf.

It climbed.

Fifty spans.

A hundred.

Two hundred.

At a thousand, the town stilled.

At five thousand, they could no longer pretend it was a machine built by the people they ate with.

It was a decision now, leaving the ground at a pace that turned moral into altitude.

At ten thousand spans, the Bridge vanished into a thin halo where blue decides it has done enough and begins practicing black.

In the harmonic throat, instruments that had names—the Varethine always name tools that carry voices—woke one by one.

Quiet-Glass cooled the air to keep numbers honest.

Echo-Reed vibrated, translating pressure into pitch.

Four-Heart braided the inputs from light, shadow, wind, and heat into a single line.

At the centre, a small, stubborn device called Kaedon's Cup waited to be filled.

Sela's team hummed the Silence First clause into the mics. It felt silly until the Bridge's hum matched them and the silliness turned sacred.

The first return came at dusk, when the sky balances its book and allows minor magics you can deny in daylight.

A low tone, then another.

Three bright.

Pause.

Two dim. Long silence.

Five.

But different.

The intervals were long where they had been short, short where they had been patient.

And under the rhythm, a low flourish—a signature.

"Not Aurethis," Tahlia said, brow furrowed under the headset.

"Aurethis with a cold. Or—" She shook her head and started again. "Aurethis from far away. Slower, older, tired."

Kaedon's Cup overflowed. The spill was light, thin as thread, gold as oath. It coiled around the throat and ran down the Bridge's ribs. On the ground, the pylons brightened by a fraction. In the Crossroads Garden, the mirror-pools held it awhile, then let it go.

The townspeople gathered in the Hall.

The Bridge relayed the sound through a reed of wire braided with patience.

It came into the room like weather entering a story about walls.

—ember—

—remember—

—carry—

Not words as a dictionary makes them.

Words as a body knows them. Bones hear meaning through the skull.

Mira's hand found Nael's. Eris closed her eyes and saw forges asleep under ash. Ryn saw a sky the colour of welding light. Liora heard a ledger, endlessly open, with no totals, only entries.

Nael raised her hand for Article One.

"Silence," she said, and the room obeyed.

They listened throughout the entire night.

The Bridge spoke only to let the sound in.

At dawn, the tone thinned and stopped, as if the River had yawned and turned to face another window.

Sela reached for the mic, eyes bright with need. Nael shook her head.

"Reciprocity," she said. "Ground first."

They put down their headsets and went to the reed-beds, the market steps, the cradles of the Flame Trees.

They listened to the tide's opinion about yesterday's cribs (favourable, with notes about spacing), to root-sap (content, requesting a different mulch), to a lattice-back (bored and itchy, requesting a child's hand on the left shoulder).

Only then did they reconvene.

"What do we send?" Liora asked, tickling dust off the Ledger with the corner of her sleeve.

"Not we," Mira said. "Who sends?"

"Four voices," Nael decided. "Pilot, engineer, poet, child."

Eris scowled. "Not a priest?"

"Faith is woven through our four," Nael said gently. "We don't need a fifth to pretend we're more reverent than we are."

They chose without drama.

Sela for the pilots.

Karo Thal for the engineers. His hands steady, his caution instructive.

Mira for the poets. Words honed enough to cut and careful enough not to.

Jace Thal-Vareth, for the children. Because he heard with his back.

They sat before the reed-mics.

The Bridge waited at the far edge of blue.

Sela went first: "We are here. We are many. We remember you without trying to own you."

Karo: "We have built a thing that can be taken apart. Say 'stop' and we will stop."

Jace (prompted only once by Mira folding his fingers around courage): "Are you tired? We can be quiet."

Mira last.

She did not read the sentence that had been pestering her.

She said something small instead: "Thank you for letting us be your children."

Nael nodded to Tahlia.

The engineer tuned the throat to give, not keep, and opened the channel for a count of five.

The Bridge sang their words without amplification, without arrogance. Wind took them and was not offended.

Then—Silence First—they closed again.

It should have ended in consensus, but the Bridge had birthed longings, and longings have sharp elbows.

Two days into the listening cycles, a petition landed on Liora's desk with a thousand names from up-coast settlements: Send a Ship. Not a glider in a river of residue, but a vessel. Small, brave, reckless to ride the echo and go see the graves of their home.

Ryn read the petition with a growth of pride and fear that made his voice sandpaper.

"They are my people," he told Nael. "And they are wrong."

Sela, who had tasted the upper air and wanted more, argued the other side.

"We cannot put a Bridge in the sky and then pretend we didn't mean bridge."

Eris hammered the table once.

"We meant listening. We wrote it down so we would remember."

A second petition arrived—fewer names, heavier grief: Let Aurethis Rest.

It came signed by farmers who had learned Illumeris' moods by kneeling in dirt, by healers who had discovered new herbs with old scents, by a quiet cluster of Solenari elders who had prayed to light for here, not there.

Mira read both petitions and said nothing until Nael looked at her the way a friend looks when they've forgiven you in advance for the thing you're about to say.

"The petitions are the same," Mira said finally. "They say, 'Please don't leave me alone here.' One asks to be taken back to the dead so the living will feel less large. The other asks the dead to stop calling so the living can learn the scale of their days."

Liora rubbed her eyes. "So, we invite them to dinner."

"Article Six," Nael said, almost smiling.

They opened the Hall, set out tables, baked too much bread.

The Listening Schools children served water and corrected adults' cadence when voices rose.

They called it a Feast of Two Longings.

Sela stood and spoke not as Pilot but as Daughter.

"My grandfather wanted to land somewhere that could forgive us. We did. The Bridge doesn't change that covenant. But it lets us touch the hem of our first history."

A farmer from Reedstone answered with hands scarred in all the honest places. "I have a child who still wakes saying the old sun's name. I want him to learn the new sun's recipes before he learns the old one's ghosts."

Arguments followed.

Good, bad, honest, performative.

Amar and Dell moved among them with chalkboards: What You Fear / What You Want / What You're Willing to Do that Costs You Something. The third column quieted the room. When it filled with offerings that looked like work, not wishes, the tone changed.

Nael stood only when the bread was nearly gone. The proper time for decisions, when appetite and rhetoric are both tired.

"The petitions are not enemies. They're hands reaching for each other across a table that used to be too long. Here is what we will do." She spoke.

She lifted a river stone and set it on the central table.

It had a dent that fit her thumb. "The Bridge will not be used to send a ship. Not now. Not until the listening ledger shows a full turning of the seasons without a single breach of the Charter. Not until Illumeris has as many names across our maps as Aurethis has across our stories."

Murmurs, but not boos.

The condition felt like a door—not locked but latched.

"And," she added, turning to the Let It Rest petitioners, "the Bridge will broadcast this place as thoroughly as it receives the other. Each listening cycle will include a reading from our ground—the river's hum, the lattice-back's breath, the names in the First Ledger spoken by children who do not know how to be pious about pronunciation. We will not send nostalgia. We will send now."

It was Eris, of course, who found the hinge. "Make the Bridge a library, not a radio," she said. "Archives travel better than orders."

Liora wrote the amendment in the margin with a sigh of relief that rustled the page.

The feast ended with the stillness song.

Not triumph.

Agreement.

Which, in Promise Bend, was triumph enough.

Weeks passed.

The Bridge learned its routes.

How to lean into the slow river in the sky without grabbing it by the throat, how to adjust its tail when the magnetosphere threw small tantrums, how to be a guest in the upper air.

Messages came.

A handful that made people sit down in the street, more that made them nod and go back to work because wonder feeds but not as well as soup.

Some were sounds: slow creaks like mountains remembering how to be magma; brittle chimes like glass bowing to heat; a soft shhh that Mira insisted was sand correcting the tide's grammar on a beach with no water.

Some were lights: threads of gold woven through black; a flare shaped like a hand and then not, because metaphor is a disease poets pass to physicists if everyone's not careful.

Once, a pattern that could only be called laughter. Ryn kicked his chair over when he heard it. Eris hid her face for a long twelve breaths.

Once, a tone that sounded exactly like the Hall of Telling at night when the door is almost closed and a child peeks back to make sure the room will still be kind tomorrow.

And once a name.

They could not agree on which name.

Each heard a different one: Sera, Lumera, Kaedon, Tavir, someone neither famous nor gone but who had held your hand on the worst day and squeezed twice.

They argued.

They stopped.

They ate.

They wrote Article Seven:

Names are for the living.

We will not hang the dead in our listening.

We will hang lanterns on the river and let them pass.

The first breach of the Charter came, predictably, from love. A storm over the north ridge knocked the Bridge sideways.

Sela's team corrected. It hummed and shrugged and went about its work. In the Hall, the listening ledger ticked on—hours sky, hours soil, hours arguing about sky and soil.

Then, one afternoon, the resonance spiked.

Not the River's tone, but something like a call. It came with a sharpness that pricked teeth. Kaedon's Cup flooded the throat with light that tasted like old metal and grief.

Sela reached reflexively for the send.

Nael's hand caught her wrist. "Silence first."

"It's calling," Sela said, voice young with tears she hadn't had time to earn.

"It's speaking," Nael corrected softly. "Not necessarily to us."

Sela's fury flashed and died. She closed her eyes. Opened them. Nodded.

They let it pass. The Bridge bowed. The light receded like a sob that decided to be breath instead. On the ridge, lightning moved its applause somewhere harmless.

That night, Sela came to Nael's office with two cups and no words. They drank. After a while, Nael said, "Thank you."

"For what?"

"For not turning our machine into a prayer we would regret."

Sela snorted a laugh. "We're not done regretting. But today I chose the slow regret instead of the fast one."

"Good," Nael said. "Slow regrets make better stories."

By the end of the first year, the Listening Ledger had pages that creaked like satisfied doors.

Illumeris entries filled more lines than Aurethis: tide behaviour under long-period pulses; lattice-back migration routes reported by children who named individuals and were corrected gently; soil moods by quadrant; flame-tree fruiting cycles; kite song forms catalogued like poetry.

The Bridge entries were fewer but heavier: a map of the echo where the Sky River brushed the magnetosphere; a catalogue of light patterns with best-guess translations; an index of griefs, because griefs deserve indices too.

All were read aloud each Week's End in the Hall, then sung once by the choirs so that memory would live in bodies, not just books.

The Feast of Two Longings became annual. Some years the Send a Ship side swelled; some years the Let it Rest side did. Most years, after bread and bickering, they wrote a new line on the Charter that made the Bridge safer for the world, not just for them.

On an evening when the bay was a sheet of hammered coin and the Flame Trees shed leaves shaped like commas, Mira stood with Nael under the tether and read the newest amendment:

Article Eight: We promise to become interesting to our descendants without making them fix us.

Mira laughed. "That one took me fifty years to shape."

Nael touched the leaf. "Worth the wait."

The Bridge drifted low at sunset, tail vanes murmuring like a tired choir after a wonderful service. The town looked up, not with fear or worship, but with the fondness reserved for tools that have learned their place.

Children chalked the day's lesson on the school wall:

LISTENING MAKES DISTANCE SMALLER / AND SHAME SMALLER / AND DAYS LARGER.

Eris and Karo finished a check on the lower pylons and sat with their feet in the river like misbehaving apprentices.

Nivara and Ryn argued amiably about a gust that had almost been a hazard until Ryn conceded the gust's right to have opinions.

Tahlia sent the last figures to the ledger and then put her slate away because numbers that sleep are nicer in the morning.

Nael walked to the Crossroads Garden.

The mirror-pools held a thin layer of gold—Aurethis had breathed in its sleep. She knelt, pressed her fingers to the water, and spoke to both suns without differentiating.

"We're still here," she said. "We're making listening a habit."

The water did not answer, but the wind did.

Small, precise, just enough to lift the hair at her temple and remind her that attention, like breath, is easiest when it's regular and rarely noticed.

She stood.

At the edge of the garden, Jace waited, taller now, shoulders learning the weight of future arguments.

"Headmistress," he said, shy with a seriousness he hadn't asked for, "if the Bridge ever learns a word we can't bear, will we stop?"

Nael considered the question the way she had learned to from elders who had built both miracles and mistakes. "We will seat sorrow," she said, "feed it, listen until we understand its accent. And then, if the word still breaks us, we will stop. We have written how."

Jace nodded as if he had been given a map with the part that said Here Be Dragons politely labelled Here Be Work.

Above them, the Bridge tugged once at its tether and settled. Out on the plain, a pair of lattice-backs stepped carefully through the grass, placing their hooves in old prints as if to keep the grammar intact. The first stars pricked the sky, indifferent and welcoming.

Nael turned toward the Hall.

Inside, Liora would close the Ledger with the gentleness of someone tucking a child in and checking the window latch twice.

Mira would sit on the step and scribble an ending that refused to end.

Sela would go to the shore and stare at the horizon until it turned its face and became dark.

Eris would laugh once, short, at a joke only tomorrow would get.

Ryn would loosen his boots and dream of the high thin air where machines and faith are indistinguishable for a breath.

Tahlia would sleep and wake with a number in her mouth that tasted like rain.

And the Bridge, obedient to its charter and its town, would bow to both suns in the only language worthy of them: listening.

CHAPTER 19

The Word We Couldn't Bear

It arrived at noon, when the town is least poetic. Pots clattered, ledgers ticked, windmills bargained with the breeze.

The Bridge was high. Tucked into that pale band where blue begins its long forgiveness into black, fulfilling Article One with disciplined quiet. Down below, the Listening Schools were in their third lesson: Ask better. Children were learning how to shape silence around questions the way potters shape air around clay.

The first warning was not sound. It was weight.

Jace Thal-Vareth, tall enough now to look most adults in the eye without apology, straightened in the schoolyard as if someone had put a book on his head.

"Headmistress?" he called, hand finding his back. "The sky just leaned."

Nael Vareth-Sael, at the chalk wall with a stub of graphite and three half-finished definitions for consent, looked up.

The tether pylons did not brighten or sing.

They stilled—the quiet of a held breath.

Across town, at the Four Flame Trees, Mira Kelen dropped her pencil and swore tenderly, the way a person swears at a child who has climbed too high and forgotten how to come down. Eris Thal set her wrench down carefully on the pylon's maintenance deck and did not move for a count of five. Sela Ryn-Kelen, in the control alcove, lifted her eyes from the ledger and saw the wind carve change shape, as if the air had found a lesson it preferred.

Nael's comm clicked. Tahlia: "Harmonic throat is warming. No external push. It's internal. The Bridge is bringing something down the line it didn't go looking for."

"Article One," Nael said, already walking. "Silence first."

"Already observed," Sela said. "We haven't opened the send. The Bridge is listening itself."

The Hall of Telling filled the way tide fills the harbour: fast, polite, inevitable. Liora stood at the ledger desk, hand on the strap; Seret took her post at the door, unarmed and unafraid; children lined the steps without being told. The lattice-backs gathered at the bluff, their fronds angled toward the tether like living weathervanes.

The first tone came like a thumb across wet crystal. The second came under it, lower, an instrument too old to have a name. The rhythm was familiar. The cadence that held their history but reversed, and then reversed again, like someone checking if the hinge still swung both ways.

Kaedon's Cup brimmed.

Light bled down the Bridge's ribs into the pylons, threading them with gold so thin you could call it imagination and not be entirely wrong.

The note climbed.

Once, twice and then broke into a syllable that wasn't sound so much as decision passing through bone.

The Hall heard different things, the way people do when one word knocks on a hundred doors at once.

Eris heard, "Stop."

Sela heard, "Hold."

Tahlia heard, "Pause."

Ryn heard, "Wait."

Liora heard, "Enough."

Mira heard, "Unmake."

Nael heard all of them and their grammar, and the grammar said: A doing must be undone.

She lifted her hand, palm down, felt sorrow, and the Hall sat without performing its grief. The pylons dimmed to listening.

"Article Six," Liora said, voice steady. "We eat first."

They laid bread on the tables and ladled stew; children poured water; no one made speeches. When hunger had been made small enough to step over without tripping, Nael stood.

"We will not decide what this word means while our blood sugar is foolish," she said, and a laugh that was both thin, grateful and moved the room from panic to work.

"Now we listen again, with quieter faces."

Sela tuned the reed-mics open by a hair.

Kaedon's Cup gave the word again, softer this time, and under it a signature flourish—two short, one long—like the grace note Kaedon had always left at the end of a cadence to remind proud people that music did not end where they liked.

Mira's knuckles whitened on the bench. "Unmake. I can't hear anything else."

Tahlia's eyes shone with a kind of pain reserved for those who fix.

"Pause is used in the engineering sense. Systems stability, resonance management. The device asks to rest."

Eris shook her head. "The river told us this once. We learned to move the tether. Now the sky says it. We learn to move our want."

Ryn scrubbed both hands over his face.

"We built a Bridge to be a good descendant. Now the ancestor asks us to put it down. Gods, I hate being loved by history."

At the far edge of the room, an older Solenari—one of the quiet ones who had taken to praying to light for here—rose unexpectedly.

Her voice was thin and true.

"When I was a child, our mirrors were told to remember everything. They became cruel. Then a girl named Lumera taught the mirrors to forget on purpose so they could keep serving. Perhaps this is the lesson in a taller key."

Nael nodded in gratitude to the old for the story, to the dead for the thread. She turned to the Charter slab at the base of the Flame Trees, traced the articles with her thumb until her skin knew them better than her mouth did, then faced the town.

"We wrote Article Five because we feared ourselves," she said. "We made the Bridge unmakeable. The word we heard—how you parse it—falls into that article's shadow. I propose we answer with what we promised when we were brave: we take the Bridge down."

Sela flinched as if struck. "For how long?"

"A season," Nael said without hesitation. "A full turning. We listen to the upper air with kites that cannot talk back. We let the ledger of ground outgrow the ledger of sky. We ask the river, the roots, the animals that stepped in our prints what changed when the Bridge learned to sing. Then we ask better questions."

Ryn exhaled a sound that might, on a less honest day, be called a laugh. "It will break me."

"It will bend you. We are a town of bending." Mira corrected softly.

Seret stepped forward.

"Bring the vote. Yes, to unmaking for a season; No, to continuing; Not Yet, if your grief needs one more bowl of soup."

They cast glass into bowls. Children carried the bowls like sacred chores, because they were. Liora tipped them, counted aloud, because secret counting had once nearly cost them a civilization.

"Yes," by a river's width.

"Not Yet," by a brook's width.

"No," by a trickle that still mattered.

Nael bowed.

Not victory, consent.

"We stop," she said. "We seat sorrow properly. Then we take out the first pins."

They did not make a parade of it. They made work.

Article Four—no single keeper—took the lead.

Sela the Pilot, Karo the Engineer, Mira the Poet, Jace the Child. Any two could halt. All four had to agree to resume.

They began at dawn under a sky that tried to be ordinary and failed because a town was telling it a secret.

Karo climbed the pylon ladders with deliberate hands and loosed the tail vanes first, singing to the bolts he had tightened with hope.

Mira stood below and read each screw, its name, as it returned to the cloth—language as oil.

Sela walked the tether line barefoot, feeling tension the way some people hear keys, and marked where the braid would sigh when freed.

Jace placed his palm against the pylon base and whispered to the note inside the metal.

"Loud-loud snap?" Seret teased gently from the ground.

"Quiet-quiet softer," Jace reported, earnest. "Like when you stop being angry, but your mouth hasn't heard."

They lowered the harmonic throat with ropes, not winches.

People who had arrived as petitioners left as riggers.

The memory-mirror panels came last, Solenari hands catching light and setting it down without bruising it.

At each stage, Liora checked the ledger. At each stage, someone, always a different someone, closed their eyes and looked like regret learning to breathe.

By afternoon, the Bridge lay on the tidal flat where it had been born.

Ribs bare, skin folded, tail unproud.

The town stood around it, hats in hands they didn't realise were clasped.

Nael stepped into the hollow where Kaedon's Cup had sat. It smelled faintly of ozone and lemon, like a storm that had done its best to be polite. She pressed her palm to the cradle and whispered, to the Bridge and to herself, "Thank you for not arguing."

Sela, with her eyes rimmed in the red that comes from not trusting your mouth to stay quiet, set a small object on the throat's rim: a glider charm, feather-thin, made of storm glass and reed. "For when you return with a better idea," she said, then turned away too fast for dignity and earned it, anyway.

They covered the parts with sailcloth.

They locked nothing.

Article Five had asked them to unbuild without a miracle; it had also taught them not to treat tools like gods.

That night, the Hall did not sing. The stillness that followed the decision is a kind of music that chooses not to be measured.

It would have been a clean lesson, neat enough for a children's book, if the world had allowed it. It made it better.

On the second day after the unmaking, a high, dry wind came down the valley with too much opinion. It pressed the river mouth inward; it pulled the bay outward; it told the market steps a joke they didn't understand. The tether pylons—unburdened, unanchored—creaked. The Four Flame Trees leaned a hair too far toward the harbour and held themselves with the dignity of elders who refuse to fall in public.

"Had we left the Bridge up," Tahlia said from the bluff, hair in her teeth, numbers in her eyes, "she would have sailed clean off her good behaviour and written herself into the reef."

"Thank the word," Mira murmured.

"You mean thank the planet," Eris said.

"I mean thank us," Seret corrected. "For listening when it was hardest."

They learned the new wind. They wrote another line in the ledger. The Not Yet bowl got a few quiet visitors who slipped their shards into Yes with no rhetoric, just relief.

The grief that remained had edges. Sela could not stop visiting the flats at dusk, toes wet, hands restless.

Ryn took to flying lower, slower, gifting his glider to thermals that did not care who had invented them.

Jace woke twice with his back thrumming, then laughed into the pillow because it was only his own heart reminding him, he had one.

Mira wrote and tore five versions of a poem called "Unmake," then left the page blank and signed the whiteness.

Nael taught more.

The Listening Schools bloomed in their season of being needed.

Children brought ground to class: a fist of soil, a reed with egg ribbons, a lattice-back frond fallen like a green hand.

They practiced translation without microphones.

"What does the soil say?"

"Sleep here, not there."

"What does the reed say?"

"Hold eggs until the wrong mouths forget the way."

"What does the frond say?"

"Do not stand where I wish to fall."

They laughed. They learned. The sky stayed where it belonged—above, mysterious, respected—not because it demanded, but because they had decided.

A week into the pause, the Bridge, resting respectfully, covered like a sleeping animal, gave one last return.

It came through Kaedon's Cup, not via the throat, a thin residual light like a memory the device had been holding for a better time.

No hum, no show. A word, folded into the simplest rhythm, spoken so quietly a child at the back had to say it aloud so the front could believe it had arrived: "Thanks."

The Hall did what Article Six had trained it for: seated sorrow.

They ate and they did not hurry joy.

Mira stood outside under the tether's simple shadow and finally wrote the line that had been following her like a stray, patient dog: when the sky asked us to undress the wonder, we folded it carefully, stitched its buttons into our pockets, and went on being a town.

She showed it to Nael.

Nael kissed her forehead without comment—old friends know when praise is an interruption.

At the season's turn, when the first cool wind found the backs of knees and made carpenters consider windows, the town gathered in the Hall with no pre-written agenda because some meetings must be allowed to invent themselves.

Liora unstrapped the ledger. "We've met the terms of the pause," she said simply. "Sky listening hours equal ground. No breaches. The Feast of Two Longings finds our tables about the same length this year. The question has not changed. Do we re-raise the Bridge?"

Silence.

Not indecision. Attention.

Sela stood and surprised herself by not immediately speaking.

She turned her palms outward. "I can want two things at once," she said. "I want the Bridge back. I want the pause again. I am willing to pay: more hours in the schools, more days with nothing but wind, fewer speeches from me."

Ryn lifted a hand. "I vote 'Yes, but slower than pride prefers.'"

Tahlia: "Yes, with a rate limiter and a child's hand on the brake."

Eris: "Yes, if we first finish the Earhouses."

This was new enough to make the room tilt. Earhouses?

Eris grinned, soot in the grin.

"Small, ground-listening pavilions. One on the reef. One in the reed beds. One under the Flame Trees. One is in the dry gullies inland. They'll hold reed-horns, mirror plates, sap gauges, and a stool that fits grief. We don't lift the Bridge until the Earhouses sing."

Mira smacked the table. "Of course. Bridges that go up require rooms that lean down."

Nael looked at the faces—the ones that had been young while learning to survive and the ones that had been old while learning to change—and felt that complicated love particular to leaders who never get what they want exactly and are spared by that fact.

"Yes," she said. "We will rebuild. Slowly. With a child holding the brake. With Earhouses teaching our knees humility. And if the word comes again—Stop, Hold, Pause, Enough, Unmake—we will answer with the courage of people who can carry both grief and awe without spilling either."

They cast the glass. Yes, won by a tether's breadth.

Not-Yet shone like restraint, not defeat.

No remained bright and small. Someone always needed to hold it, so the rest remembered how.

They built the Earhouses first.

On the reef, a low dome of glass and reed, walls humming with wave grammar. In the reeds, a long, narrow shelter on stilts, steps that taught ankles caution and hearts patience. Under the Flame Trees, a bench shaped like a question. In the inland gullies, a wind-throat cut into stone, tuned by children who had learned to hear dust.

People went there in pairs: pilot with farmer, poet with welder, child with anyone who would let them lead.

They wrote in the ear books: river said Later, wind said Lower, root said Cool, sand said Wait.

Those pages were read on market mornings before prices; shouted from pylons before lifts; whispered to newborns before names.

Only after the Earhouses had taught the town a new set of courtesies did they return to the flat with uncovered ribs and folded tail.

They raised the Bridge like you rehang a bell in a chapel you've repaired by hand.

At half height, Jace lifted his palm. "Brake," he said, shy only out of habit, and Sela smiled and did it, eyes wet, because power that obeys a child on purpose is a better invention than any engine.

At full height, the Bridge bowed to both suns and kept its chartered silence until the Feast.

Then it listened—no send—for a single cycle, and when the word arrived again—softer, more like thanks than command—the town answered by seating joy, which is harder to do than the other thing and therefore better practice.

Nael walked to the Crossroads Garden and found Evara there, older, carved elegantly by years that did not apologise for themselves. They stood together, watching the mirror-pools hold a thin skin of gold and then let it go.

"Did we choose correctly?"

Nael asked, knowing the question is the work, not the answer.

Evara tapped her stick, smiled the slow way of the satisfied and critical. "We chose together," she said. "Correctness is what you do next."

They stood for a while in a silence that was not empty. Up on the bluff, the Listening Schools rang the soft bell that meant come hear what the water learned today. Out on the plain, lattice-backs stepped where they wanted and sometimes where you hoped; they had their own charter, unwritten and binding.

Above, the Bridge held its line like a thread between two sleeves of a coat that finally fit.

In the Hall, Liora closed the ledger on a season that had not broken them and wrote one more promise in the margin, because margins had become the place where truth liked to sit:

We promise to let difficult words teach us kinder hands.

The wind approved, which is to say: it did nothing unusual and was therefore kind. The town slept.

The stars took their turns.

Far off, beyond courtesy and near to love, a faint echo moved along a river that was not water and remembered a people who had learned, at last, how to hear "unmake" and survive the lesson.

CHAPTER 20

The Third Light

The decision to send a ship again came not from hunger or nostalgia. It came from practice. From years of listening had made the town fluent in patience; the Bridge rose and bowed by charter; the Earhouses murmured ground-truth into every plan.

When the vote came, quiet, complicated, kind, it said: one vessel, with brakes on the child's side, with the Bridge as its teacher, with Article Six in its pocket.

The ship was small as promises and built like them too: strong in its joints, light in its pride.

They named her Crosswind Promise.

Sela Ryn-Kelen would pilot.

Karo Thal would keep the ship honest.

Mira Kelen would carry the words that don't fit on slates.

Jace Thal-Vareth, who'd grown into his height as if good posture were an ethic, would sit at the fourth seat, feet on the brake if anyone forgot what Stop can save.

Nael Vareth-Sael stayed, by choice.

Someone had to tend the long listening so that leaving would not start a habit. She stood under the Four Flame Trees as the ship lifted, her hand on the ledger, her face turned to the sky that had learned their names.

"Silence first, then speech, then correction," she said into the comm, the cadence of the schools braided with Kaedon's old music. "Come home with listening, not with proof."

"Understood," Sela replied.

The Crosswind Promise rose, caught the upper thermals, and let the Bridge hand it to the resonance layer where the Sky River's echo grazed the magnetosphere like a fingertip flirting with water.

They did not force the door.

They hummed three bright, pause, two dim, long silence, five, and the passage accepted them with the weary good humour of an old road that still took travellers because roads are stubbornly hospitable.

The stars rearranged, as they had once before, but the crew no longer called that magic.

It was familiarity.

The physics of practiced grief.

The helix unscrolled, folded, tightened—and then let go.

The ship dropped out of the river into a night full of blue gloaming and a medium yellow sun like clean honey.

The new star was not new.

It was a G-class, steady and middle-aged, burning with the confidence of neither youth nor decline.

"Milky Way," Karo breathed—the word a lesson from their charts rather than a memory. "We're back in the old long river."

Sela eased them into the high dark above a planet that filled the forward view with oceans and continents and a necklace of clouds that decided weather with more opinion than Illumeris ever had.

A single large moon hung white at a respectful distance, tidally tethered in a dance that spoke of stability.

"Third planet," Tahlia's voice came over the thin Bridge-line relays, delayed by courtesy, not distance. "Spectral class verified. Magnetosphere robust. Ozone intact. Auroras are like poetry."

The Crosswind Promise pivoted, axes steady, instruments greedy and polite.

Mass: 1.01 of Illumeris.

Radius: a hair larger.

Gravity: kind to bone.

Day length: just under 24 standard hours; the number felt good in the mouth.

Axial tilt: ~23.5°. Seasons promised rather than threatened.

Cycle: the long loop: ~365 days.

Atmosphere: 78% nitrogen, ~21% oxygen, trace argon, CO_2 whispering at the edge of arguments; water vapor good enough to kiss.

Continents sprawled like the story's maps tell: one long spine stitched with mountains; one continent cradled by two oceans; one that looked like a hand splayed into islands; one wrapped in ice at the bottom like a doctrine; one at the top shingled with pack and promise.

Rolls turned in the seas, swimmer's wrists in slow motion. Jet streams traced cursive scripts across latitudes. Biomes gleamed: equatorial rainforests dark and wet, deserts the colour of old metal, mid-latitude grasslands combed by wind, boreal forests like thought made tree.

"Home to something," Mira said reverently. "Home to many somethings."

Then the instruments went wild.

Not with flare or flux, not with radiation or rock.

With a signal.

It came first as broadband snow that wasn't snow at all— radio hiss stitched with teeth.

Then narrow-band whispers piled on top of each other until the spectrograph looked like a city seen through rain.

Carrier waves at crisp, regular intervals. Frequency-modulated voices crowded into bands. Pulses that counted time for machines in orbit and on the ground. Chirp radars painting the sky.

Beacon identifiers calling themselves by names: VORs, TACANs, GPS pseudo-random codes, timing ticks precise enough to keep promises.

Mira put her hand to her mouth. "They're talking."

"Not to us," Sela said, smiling in the place where awe and discipline shake hands. "To themselves. That's better."

Karo tuned down: 3 to 30 megahertz—HF—and the world answered with skips and fades, storm static, and voices that rode the ionosphere between night and day. He tuned up: VHF and UHF, where airfields and ships negotiated edges, where weather told pilots how to be cautious, where satellites spoke in square packets. He looked higher: L-band timing, S-band telemetry. He looked sideways: microwave backscatter that spelled microwave ovens and radar dishes and rain.

And under it, music.

It arrived smudged by Doppler and atmosphere, fractured by geography, braided by a thousand transmitters.

A snatch of strings here, a trumpet there, drums that did not apologise for their insistence, a woman's voice that slid across a scale like a river remembering rock.

Laughter.

News that did not sound like facts so much as weather about people.

Advertisements that used persuasion like percussion.

Languages: sibilants and clicks and vowels held long; stress-timed and syllable-timed cadences; tongues that loved consonants the way some people love spices.

"Third planet," Mira whispered. "Third light."

Sela held them high, darked the hull, and asked the new world its night-side.

The ship obliged: the planet rolled, and the dark took shape—cities blooming in constellations of sodium and LED, continents veined in light where roads ran, coasts beading like necklaces. The terminator moved, and dawn poured across a desert so flat it looked like silence, across mountains that dialled sunrise into awe, across archipelagos that stitched together boats and homes and faith.

Karo's screen blinked.

"We're painted. Primary radar. Civil, not military—sweep speed benign. They can see we exist as weather with opinions." He said calmly.

"Keep our cross-section polite," Sela said. "We are a bird too far to eat."

Jace leaned closer to the glass, eyes wide. "They're sending so much hello without knowing."

"Listening first," Sela reminded, and he nodded as if he'd moved his hand to the brake and discovered it already there.

They catalogued the New World.

Not as conquerors, not even as guests, but as neighbours who've discovered someone lives behind the hedge and have learned their schedule before choosing a time to knock.

Oceans: salinity ~35‰; large western boundary currents like rivers turned into walls; upwelling zones stippling the surface with plankton wealth—chlorophyll flares bright as a meadow in space. Seas within continents counting themselves like pockets. Tides tugged by that faithful moon; a system where the tide rotates around a central point of little to no tidal range, points, like hinges.

Continents:

• One long spine (call it by its ancient names later) with eastern coasts bitten into by rias and drowned valleys; broad interior plains clothed in grain and grass; a western mountain chain reaching into the jetstream to make weather think twice.

• Another cradle of two oceans, heart patterned in river deltas that braided trade and history and silt.

- An old plateau that sang stone, its shield wearing deserts and scrub like ethics.

- An island continent that carried marsupials in its fields of evolution, ringed by reefs bright enough to teach colour new things.

- A polar continent that hid mountains under ice two kilometres thick, storing ancient sky in air bubbles like a meticulous archivist.

Biota: spectral lines from canopy and grasslands and algae dancing in an unembarrassed green; methane plumes above wetlands where life digests itself politely; dust blooms out of deserts that fertilize forests an ocean away—world as argument that nourishes.

Weather: cyclones swirling names into coastlines; monsoons doing the old bargaining between sea and land; Rossby waves rolling like patient grammar; atmospheric rivers—long plumes of water knitting mountains to oceans in rain.

Magnetosphere: bow shock like a shield; auroral ovals, burning curtains into the polar dark; Van Allen belts like stern warnings.

Orbitals: a cloud of artificial satellites—navigation, imaging, weather, talk—moving on Keplerian chores, whispering to ground with the efficiency of bees. Debris, too—unintentional constellations that promised the new world had already learned a few regrets you can see from space.

Sela watched the sweep of a large, phased array on the nightside, the disciplined blink of a geostationary ring.

"They walk in the sky," she murmured. "Carefully and often."

"And they listen," Mira said, head cocked as a chorus rose—a long, sustained tone, modulated, purposeful.

Deep Space Network?

A cousin, at least. Big dishes turning like slow thoughts, ears pointed outward.

Karo toggled a filter, then another.

The tone cleaned.

He brought it down into sound range, and they heard it like wind over copper. Someone, somewhere in the third world, was listening to the universe, not because it answered, but because it might.

Sela smiled. "Kin."

"Rules," Jace said quietly, reminding them and himself.

"Rules," Sela agreed. "Article One: silence first."

They waited.

One orbit.

Two.

They sampled coastal air without dipping, tasting salt and industrial volatiles and pollen that made Karo sneeze from memory alone.

They skimmed Nightside again.

Down there, storms struck bright forked signatures.

Airliners stitched safe lines between cities.

Ships wrote slow Morse across oceans; AIS pings stacked like patient groceries.

The Crosswind Promise could have answered every hello.

She didn't.

She turned her dish outward and sent a single note.

Not toward the ground, but toward the Bridge riding their home sky far away.

"We are at the Third Light," Sela spoke.

"We have arrived at a habitable world in the Milky Way, third planet from a G-class star, one large moon, vigorous magnetosphere, biomes abundant. And the air hums with signals. Radio, radar, music, talk. They are not waiting. They are doing."

Nael's reply, delayed and perfect: "Then we will not arrive as an interruption. Bring back listening."

They mapped one place to stand near—not the biggest city, not the quietest wild. A mid-latitude coast on the night side where city light met estuary and forest, where wind carried salt and leaf together, where planes crossed high lanes and fishing boats idled under the mouths of gulls. The ship dipped to edge-of-sky, Kármán's old argument, and rode along the line where re-entry is a choice, not a mistake.

"Not landing," Sela murmured to the ship. "Just closer."

The signal forest thickened.

FM stations stacked like market stalls; AM towers murmured like snoring giants; cellular bands trilled; microwave backhaul stitched sub-cloud like spider silk. Karo's spectrum analyser bloomed.

Jace, eyes closed, listened for the shape beneath the noise—the cadence of a people.

He found it where he always does in the gaps.

Between weather reports and pop songs. Between laughing commercials and the voice that said, quietly, across a quiet band: "Is anyone on this frequency? We're safe for now."

"They argue. They love. They warn. They feed," he said, translating overwhelm into nouns.

Mira held the page steady on her knee, as if any line might run away if she failed to be furniture. "The word is plural," she said. "So must we be."

Karo's scope chirped. "We're lit by a tracking radar that knows what it's doing," he said. "If we cross one more line, someone will come and ask for our papers."

"Then we stay in courtesy, not permission, and never try to fake permission," Sela replied. "We'll leave them something to find if they're looking up."

"What?" Jace asked, braced on his brake.

Trust now was a reflex, not a lesson.

Mira unfolded a small reed disk, etched with Kaedon's backward cadence and Nael's six laws, in a language that used pictures first and math second and music always. The disk held chlorophyll spectra and hydrogen lines and a map not of where to go, but of how to ask to be welcome.

Around the rim was a promise written in numbers. The one dialect that tends not to lie when it behaves itself: silence first, then speech, then correction.

"Leave it in the high air," Mira said. "A buoy. Not a rock. If they want it, they can fetch it. If they don't, the wind has a pretty toy."

Karo used a reaction puff to lower a small aerostat to the upper stratosphere.

It carried the disk, and a mirror tag no bigger than a hand, tuned to glint a tiny, polite flash at certain radar paints. Not enough to startle, enough to invite curiosity. The payload rode the breath of the world, drifting down a millimetre at a time, bound to be found by a weather balloon, a curious radio club, or a student out staring at the sky with the dangerous habit of wonder.

"Now we leave," Sela said. "Before we feel clever."

They lifted, gliding to the rim of the atmosphere until blue turned to the tired black that forgives ships. The planet curved beneath them, whole and busy. Sela turned once to look: a storm the size of a nation spinning like slow punctuation; a river writing itself to sea; a chain of islands arguing their names with tides.

"Third Light," she whispered, because names spoken twice sometimes place themselves better. "We will not treat you like a mirror."

The Crosswind Promise eased back into the helix, letting the Bridge tug them into the old cadence: three bright, pause, two dim, long silence, five. Behind them, the new world went on with its day: talking to itself, listening outward, making breakfast.

They fell into the familiar wide of Illumeris under a dawn that had missed them politely and was glad to see their shape back. The ship kissed the bluff with practiced gratitude. Promise Bend, larger now and not embarrassed about it, gathered like weather when something good comes home.

The report took days to write and was told many times.

Each audience catching a different shimmer from a story too big to sit still.

In the Hall, Liora read the Ledger: mass, tilt, day, year, oceans, gyres, deserts, storms. The Earhouses reported ground-truth in parallel: reefs calving, reeds ribboning, gullies filling; because the habit they were proudest of was the one that kept near drowning in far.

Article Six did its work: before they argued about contact strategies, they ate in a circle and seated sorrow for what news of another home can wake. Elders cried neat tears. Children grinned with their entire faces. Seret poured water like truce. Eris laughed once and then helped someone carry bowls because being useful is a better drug than awe.

When the time came to choose their next habit, they did it in sentences that had learned to be useful.

"We do not announce," Nael said. "We prepare."

"We build an Earhouse in the sky," Eris added—an orbital listening buoy that stays a guest at the edge of sound.

"We translate our Charter into pictures and mathematics and rhythm, then give it to the Bridge to sing into the dark," Mira said.

"We teach our children how to explain us without apology and how to ask permission without surrender," Sela said.

"And we wait for their curiosity to find the aerostat and the mirror tag, not because we're timid, but because consent is the first architecture of friendship," Karo finished.

They voted in glass.

The Not-Yet bowl filled with enough shards to make the Yes brave instead of fast. The No glinted like flint. The edge you keep to cut bad rope if needed.

After, as lanterns took up their night work on the river and lattice-backs made pillows of their own fronds, Nael, and Mira climbed to the bluff.

"What will they call us?" Mira asked, more curiosity than worried.

"Late," Nael said, and smiled. "And then, neighbour, if we do this right."

A thin ion thread from the Bridge brushed her wrist.

She turned and spoke into it.

The message for Aurethis, for Illumeris, for the Third Light and any other listening patience braided between stars.

WE FIND YOU.

WE WILL NOT HURRY YOU.

OUR HANDS ARE FULL OF WORK AND OPEN FOR FRIENDSHIP.

WE BRING LISTENING.

On the ridge behind them, the Listening School rang the soft bell. Children wrote the day's lesson on the board:

WHEN YOU HEAR MANY HELLOS, ANSWER WITH ONE GOOD QUESTION.

Far away in the Milky Way, a weather technician would one day retrieve a balloon payload, fingers chapped, eyes bright, and find a reed disk that smelled faintly of sun-warmed plant and ship. They would hold it to light, watch the hydrogen line mark its universal place, trace a spiral that was not a command but an invitation, and hear—if they were the sort of person who still stood still sometimes—the rhythm three bright, pause, two dim, long silence, five.

They would take it to a room with dishes that looked outward. Mouths would argue. Eyes would soften. A new habit would begin.

Back at Promise Bend, Liora closed the Ledger of the First Era with the gentleness of someone tucking in a child and checking the window latch twice. On the last line, in a hand that would be quoted and mocked and underlined, she wrote:

Between suns, we learned to be citizens of listening.

Under the third light, we will try to be good neighbours.

The Bridge, obedient to charter and love, bowed to Aurethis and Illumeris and the Third Light in the only language worthy of them.

Listening.

And the wind, which has always been an excellent editor, approved.

Epilogue

They saw each other first. Not in speeches or in myths, but in the clean arithmetic of optics: a glint from high air, answered by a blink from ground. The aerostat-buoy that carried Mira's reed disk rode a bright winter jet and drifted down into the hands of weather people who still believed in wonder.

Days later, on the far side of the planet, a coastal array of dishes turned like thoughtful flowers, and a low-power laser pulsed up through the troposphere toward the Bridge:

WE SEE YOU.
DO YOU HEAR US?

Promise Bend answered the way they had practiced.
Silence first, then music.

The Bridge returned a narrow beam that laid numbers on the wind: the hydrogen line, the count to five, the geometry of a circle shown three different ways, and then Kaedon's cadence, three bright, pause, two dim, long silence, five, wrapped around six simple laws:

Listen. Ask. Wait. Consent.
Stop when asked. Come gently.
The reply came in layers.

First, mathematics: primes, constants, a shared sky drawn in frequency instead of ink.

Then, maps: of orbits, of weather, of coastlines that looked like hands.

Then, rules: a short charter about airspace and quarantine, about bringing no hunger and leaving with no soil.

Finally, an invitation:

LET US SPEAK SLOWLY.
WE WILL MEET YOU WHERE THE SEA GREETS THE CITY.

Negotiations spun like a bridge being braided.

Thread over thread, tension and give.

They happened in three languages at once: numbers, pictures, and rhythm.

Promise Bend sent a child's sketch of their handshake: palm open, nothing hidden. The Third World returned a video of sailors saluting the horizon and a farmer holding up loam, as if to say:

We know what it means to carry ground in your hands.

They invented protocols together.

The Place: a broad, sunlit headland on a large continent surrounded by water, where ocean scent walked easily into town. The charts called it a parliamentary capital; the pilots called it a good wind; the poets would later call it the Edge That Introduced Us.

The Approach: Crosswind Promise would descend at dawn along a corridor plotted with the locals' own radars, transponder talking in the new agreed code.

No supersonics. No drama. A landing you could read a book to.

The Terms: no samples taken, none given; no weapons, none needed; Article Six carried in every pocket, when sorrow arrives, seat it, because any first meeting risks a little.

The Words: each side would bring four.

Pilot. Engineer. Poet. Child.

And a fifth who could say yes on behalf of many without forgetting they were made of one.

Acceptance sounded ordinary:

COME. WE'LL PUT THE KETTLE ON.

Dawn bent itself over the headland.

On one side, the ocean shouldered the rocks; on the other, a city lifted glass and stone into a sky salted with gulls.

Flags woke on their poles.

News drones held a respectful distance.

Somewhere, coffee made its argument for civilization.

Crosswind Promise came over the sea—hull dulled to kindness, vanes quiet, heat signature polite.

People on foreshore paths stopped the way people do when a story they were told as children steps out of the book and asks about the weather.

The ship touched down on a pad painted with a circle and a cross, the sort of sign that reminds pilots to trust rectangles; her skids kissed concrete the way you greet a sleeping dog. The wind applauded without getting up. Hatches sighed.

Ramps unfolded with the grace of practiced humility.

Sela Ryn-Kelen walked first, palms open, eyes ready for both joy and correction.

Karo Thal came after, hands loose at his sides like a man meeting a river he hopes will forgive his boots.

Mira Kelen carried a satchel of reed and glass—the portable promise of stories.

Jace Thal-Vareth kept one hand near the brake lever inside the hatch, because lessons are only real when they can be reached.

They waited and a small motorcade rolled up from the city in quiet cars, open faces.

At its centre stepped a person in a dark, neat suit that couldn't quite hide the salt on their cuffs.

A handful of aides fanned out and then remembered to make room for the view.

Cameras exhaled.

The gulls remained unimpressed.

The person walked forward with the unhurried confidence of someone who has shaken many hands without forgetting what hands are for.

They stopped a respectful span away, let the wind decide the last step, then closed it with a smile that belonged to the day more than to any office.

"I'm Prime Minister Alana Pierce," they said, vowels set wide by sun and sea, consonants clipped like sails before a gust.

The accent carried a friendly tilt, syllables leaning on each other as if keen to share the load.

They extended a hand. "G'day. Welcome. We're chuffed you made the trip. Let's have a yarn."

Sela grinned without rehearsal and took the hand.

Warm.

Dry.

Humans with a local spelling.

"We've brought listening," she said.

"Brilliant," the Prime Minister replied—bril-yint, the r soft, the i smiling—"because we've brought tea and questions."

Laughter moved through the gathered crews and guards the way relief travels in a crowd: quickly, quietly, making room for breath.

Protocol officers stepped forward, placed small microphones on collars, and then stepped back because this kind of moment doesn't like chaperones.

They did not rush speeches.

They let seeing finish its work.

Up close, faces lose their myth and find their persons.

Sela noticed the Prime Minister's weathered knuckles; the Prime Minister noticed the callus on Karo's thumb from bolts that had been persuaded into good behaviour; Mira noticed a junior aide mouthing her poems' lines from a screen as if rehearsal could make courage permanent; Jace noticed a child behind the rope line counting to five over and over, little fingers bright with chalk dust.

"Shall we?" the Prime Minister said, and the small party walked toward a tent whose sides were up so the sea could listen, and the city could hear.

The first messages were simple and kind.

We came because our star dimmed.

We stayed because your sky called.

We won't take what isn't offered.

We carry a ledger that lists ground before sky.

We have rules about stopping.

We pack our sorrow in bowls.

The permissions were measured and generous.

You may walk on our shore, not our hospitals.

You may ask our engineers how, not our farmers why.

You may bring one seed in a story, none in soil.

You may teach a song; we will teach you to queue.

The negotiations were a good afternoon's work, which is to say they were long enough to matter and short enough to preserve goodwill.

The Prime Minister's team asked for data sharing bounded by common sense; Promise Bend's delegation asked for consent bounded by time, not fatigue.

A doctor proposed a joint quarantine ritual involving handwashing and a slightly ridiculous hat no one was forced to wear; a poet proposed they both agree to apologise quickly if they forgot themselves.

The solicitors translated poetry into clauses with admirable restraint.

Acceptance did not arrive as a stamp or a trumpet.

It arrived as a tray: ceramic mugs, honey, lemon, three kinds of biscuits, and a pitcher of water whose condensation drew maps on the tablecloth.

A staffer with a studied casualness poured first for those who had not travelled, then for those who had—a protocol the Prime Minister explained with a grin as "our way of reminding the hosts they're still at home."

Sela lifted her cup. "To neighbours," she said.

"Neighbours," the Prime Minister echoed, the word softened at the edges by their seaside vowels: nay-buhs.

"To slow neighbours who stay for tea."

They shook hands again, the way people do after a contract is signed and before the work begins.

Outside the tent, the ocean leaned in to hear better, and the city remembered its chores.

Above, the Bridge held to its orbit and said nothing, which was the most eloquent thing it could do.

That evening, as gulls argued punctuation over the headland and the city lit itself like careful jewellery, Crosswind Promise opened her hatch to a small group of scientists, singers, and schoolchildren with packed lunches and questions that had not been improved by committee.

On the grass below, kids traced the hull's shadow with chalk until it looked like a ship drawn by a planet.

Later still, when the speeches had been put to bed and the last microphone had stopped trying to be helpful, Sela stepped out under the southern stars with the Prime Minister.

The wind smelled of eucalyptus and salt.

Somewhere, a tram sighed.

Somewhere else, a pub laughed.

"Does it feel," the Prime Minister asked, "like you've come home?"

Sela watched the surf write and erase the shoreline with enviable confidence. "It feels," she said, "like we've come next door, and the neighbour opened the door with a cup in their hand."

"Good," the Prime Minister replied, vowels softening into night. "We're better at kettles than at trumpets. Tomorrow we'll argue affectionately about bureaucracy. Tonight, we'll let the water introduce us." As they tilted their heads toward the sea.

They stood in companionable quiet while the waves did exactly that.

Above them, satellites crossed like unhurried thoughts.

Far away at Promise Bend, the Four Flame Trees shed a few leaves, and Liora wrote one more line in the Ledger's margin:

First contact, third planet, large water-ringed continent.

We saw, we spoke, we asked.

They said yes.

We shook hands and laughed at an accent, then learned it meant the same thing our wind means: you are welcome if you come gently.

Under the third light, the handshake held.

And because both sides had practiced listening long enough to trust it, the genuine work—the slow, neighbourly work—could begin.

About the Author

José F. Nodar

Flung into one of life's biggest challenges at just eleven, José's story began in Havana, Cuba. The Cuban Revolution forced him onto a plane alone, landing him at an orphanage in a small Georgia town called Washington. Reuniting with his parents wouldn't happen until he was eighteen, a high school graduate in Atlanta.

Business Administration became his focus at Georgia State University. From there, he navigated the world of finance, first at the First National Bank of Atlanta (now Wells Fargo) and later as a project manager in financial consulting. These roles took him across the United States, Europe, and even Australia.

It was in Camden, New South Wales, Australia, that a spark ignited José's creative side. A writers' group became the launching pad for his debut novel, and soon, his mind birthed Danny Monk, his first major character.

But José's life isn't all about writing. When he's not crafting captivating stories, you might find him at the local mall, observing the world and gathering inspiration for future characters. Away from his computer, he dives into books or enjoys long strolls around Spring Farm.

Other books by José F. Nodar

English

Books, Pens & Larceny

Mending Hearts at Crystal Cove

A Love Finally Spoken

The Legacy Compass

The Universe Between Us

The Time Bus

Somewhere in Time

SEX

The Clause that Killed Him

The Compass Legacy

The Teacher's Assistant

Love in Stereo

Whispers From My Wife

Stories to Share with My Partner Book 1

Stories to Share with My Partner Book 2

Stories to Share with My Partner Book 3

Stories to Share with My Partner Book 4

Stories to Share with My Partner Book 5

Stories to Share with My Partner Book 6

Stories to Share with My Partner Book 7

Stories to Share with My Partner Book 8

Stories to Share with My Partner Book 9

Stories to Share with My Partner Book 10

Stories to Share with My Partner Book 11

Stories to Share with My Partner Book 12

Spanish

- Cuentos Para Compartir con Mi Pareja Libro 1
- Cuentos Para Compartir con Mi Pareja Libro 2
- Cuentos Para Compartir con Mi Pareja Libro 3
- Libros, Bolígrafos y Hurto
- Reparando Corazones en Crystal Cove
- Un Amor Finalmente Declarado
- El Autobús del Tiempo
- Una Noche de Amor